BROKEN TRUTH

MELISSA HUIE

Editorial provided by Renita Lofton McKinney from A Book A Day Author Services – www.abookaday.net

Editing and Formatting:

Amy Briggs, Briggs Editorial Services, www.editsbyamy.com

Cover Design:

Robin Harper, Wicked by Designwww.wickedbydesigncovers.com and Marisa-Rose Black, covermedarling.com

Front Cover Photography:

JW Photography – www.jwphotographicart.com

Models:

Morgan Boyd – Morgan Instagram - @_moalisa

Joshua Sargent – Instagram - @sargjosh

PLAYLIST

Broken Redemption Playlist
https://bit.ly/42XM4xF

Orange Blossoms – GoldFord
When It's Gone – Bernz, Kiddo
Sleep with the Stars – The Witching Hour
Everywhere I go – FNKHOUSER
Shaking Cages – Silent Theory
OHMAMI – Chase Atlantic
I Did Something Bad – Taylor Swift
Sinner – DEZI
Poison Ivy – Hemi Moore
Where Are You? – Elvis Drew, Avivian
Outta My Head – Omido, Rick Jansen, Ordell
Surround Sound – JID, 21 Savage, Baby Tate
Styrofoam - $uicideboy$
Shadows – Ryan Jesse
Ni X El PUTXS – Ryan Castro, Kris R
Sneaky – 21 Savage

Glock In My Lap – 21 Savage, Metro Boomin
Way Down We Go –
La Canción – J Balvin, Bad Bunny
MONACO – Bad Bunny
TEETH - WesGhost(feat Diggy Graves)
Chokehold – Sleep Token

THE BROKEN ROAD SERIES

(To be read in Order)

SENSITIVITY WARNING

This series contains themes of sexual assault and human trafficking of adults and children, along with depictions of drugs, violence, and graphic sex. Reader discretion is advised.

To all of my readers, family and friends who pushed me, supported me, and encouraged me through the years.
Thank you.
xoxo

PROLOGUE

Ten years ago

THERE WERE two sides to every story. Just like there were two sides of me.

I lived in two different worlds. My everyday life was both structured and noisy. I was lonely in a city of millions. Tempered and molded, I fit into a box to be the person my parents wanted me to be. My everyday life felt like a lie.

But every chance I could, I escaped.

I was able to be free. For the briefest time, I could be the person I wanted to be.

Sayulita, Mexico was my home away from home. A place where I could find myself, where I could live. My grandmother's family originally settled there. My grandmother was born there, but grew up as a child of two countries, living the majority of her life in Detroit, Michigan. She met my grandfather while working at the steel mill. Once she and my grandfather retired, and my father and siblings had grown up and left their nest, they moved back to her home of Sayulita, what once was a small fishing village on the Pacific side of Mexico. Sayulita was my oasis, where I was free to explore my interests and be whomever I wanted to be. At least for the summer anyway.

Every time I arrived on the sands of that beautiful beach, I felt alive. At home. And most importantly, like I freaking mattered.

"Mija, what time are you coming home?" my abuela asked, as I walked through the hallway. I pulled up short and my bare feet almost tripped over the multi-color rugged laid out over the cream-colored terracotta tile floor. I should have known she would have heard me. The woman was in her late sixties and her hearing was as sharp as my mother's when I tried to sneak out as a teenager. I wasn't necessarily trying to sneak out, but I also wasn't very open on my whereabouts. It would then lead to more unnecessary questions, like who I was going with or where I was going. I poked my head into the airy living room. Abuela was barely paying attention to me, her focus primarily on a telenovela.

"I'll be home late, Abuelita," I replied nonchalantly.

"Remind me tomorrow, we need to go to Sammy's. They forgot my fish order and I was planning to make pescado zarandeado," she called. While I loved how she was going to make my favorite fish dish, dinner the next day was beyond my focus at the moment.

"Of course, Abuelita." I grabbed my bag and moved toward the door.

"Oh Evie?" Her voice carried through the open hallway. I stopped right as my hand grasped the knob of the door.

"Si?" I replied with a sigh. I strained to keep my patience in check, but I was already running late.

"Siempre puedes traer al niño a casa contigo. Me gustaría

conocer al chico con el que has estado saliendo." I could hear her sly smirk from the other room. *Fuck! How did she know?*

"I don't know what you're talking about, Abuelita. There's no boy for you to meet," I replied dutifully. Of course not. Because I'm all man, Bebe. I could hear his dirty voice in my ear and almost shivered.

"I may be sixty-seven years old but I'm not blind nor am I dumb. You think I haven't lived in this town long enough for me to have friends? Friends who call me when they see my beautiful nieta canoodling with some gringo at the beach?" I heard her tennis shoes squeaking across the floor as she made her way over to me. My face flamed in embarrassment.

I turned and watched her come closer. "Tienes amigas muy entrometidas," I snarked with amusement, my hands on my hips. She laughed, her salt and pepper poof wobbled as she shook her head, her hot pink cane keeping her steady as she made her way over to me.

"Nah, mija. My friends are not nosy. They are happy to see you happy. They haven't seen you since last summer, and even then, your head was in the books. They're seeing you with a smile now. They like it."

I heaved another sigh. The last thing I needed was for people to go telling Abuela about my business. Because if it's getting back to her, then it could be getting back to my parents.

Abuela put her gnarled dark brown hands on my cheeks and looked up at me. Even though I was five-foot-three on a good day, my abuela barely broke five feet. Her face grew grave. "You deserve your fun. This is your season to shine like the sun before you go back to the gloomy weather." I clasped my hands over hers, feeling the softness of her wrinkled skin. "I want to meet this boy."

"He's just a tourist," I murmured. He was actually more

than that. So much more than that. But my heart sank because I knew our relationship had an expiration date.

Her beautiful brown eyes looked at me sadly. "A tourist is someone temporary. Sometimes, we just need temporary."

"Abuela! Are you encouraging me to have a fling? I am not a hussy!" I exclaimed softly, in faux shock. She rolled her eyes at me in exasperation. Despite the heavy conversation, I grinned at her reaction. I loved riling her up.

"Por el amor de dios. My dear nieta. You're eighteen years old. You have the rest of your life to live within the confines of adulthood. Soon you'll be going back home," she said with remorse. Despite being my father's mother, she was very much against the life he chose. "You're going to look back and wish you did so much more. Do not live with regret. Living your best life sometimes means saying Joder. Aún estás viva, carino. Vívelo libre mientras puedas," she exclaimed. I giggled every time she said "fuck it" but her telling me to live my life free while I can hit me in my heart.

I grasped her hands. "Si, Abuelita. Maybe I will introduce you before he leaves."

She smirked. "He's a good boy, yes?"

My face flushed with all the dirty things we've done. I still maintained my v-card, but if I had the choice, it would be his.

"Yes, he's a good boy. I promise. He's kind, and charming, and he makes me laugh," I replied softly.

"And you're feeling okay? You're all better?" she asked, as worry came across her face.

I sighed and gave her a big smile. "Yes. I'm one hundred percent back to normal."

"Good. Go see your friend." She paused to look out the window. "Just be careful. A storm is coming through super early tomorrow. Try to be home before then."

"I will." I kissed her weathered cheek and hurried out the

door. Despite his asking, I never gave him my number and I didn't ask for his. I had no way of knowing if he would have waited, but I hoped he did.

Thinking of his brown eyes and dimpled smile made my heart flutter. My steps quickened as I hurried down the brick and dirt street to our meeting spot on the beach. My tangerine-colored sundress swished around my legs, and my knotless braids bounced off my back as I dodged the people in my way.

I didn't want to be a sweaty mess when I finally met up with him, but I didn't want to miss this chance. We met early last week while I was volunteering with Campamento Tortuguero Sayulita, a sea turtle educational community project. He was on leave from the U.S. Navy and I was talking with a group of tourists about how to protect the sea turtles from poaching. He joined my group, made me laugh and asked me out. Ever since then, we had spent some time together every day.

The first time he kissed me was under the stars on the beach, after we watched the hatchlings make their way to open water. The day before, we did a bit of paddle boarding then had ice cream at the on the beach. , I wanted to take him to the plaza. I hoped to have dinner and drinks, maybe a little dancing. The anticipation made me giddy. Once I made it to the corner of Av. del Palmar, I saw him. My heart leaped into my throat.

His smile widened, and the dimple in his cheek more pronounced. I couldn't help but smile back.

"Hi, Cole."

ONE

Cole

I tended to think of myself as pretty brave. Nothing phased me. I'd jumped out of helicopters into the desert in the dark of night. I'd faced down mercenaries in the jungles of Columbia and Cambodia. I'd climbed up to the base camp of Mt. Everest and cage-dived with great white sharks off the coast of Cape Town, South Africa.

I looked in the face of my fears and gave it the middle finger.

But nothing had ever made me more scared than those two words.

"I'm pregnant."

My heart immediately dropped, and my stomach went sour. For the briefest of moments, true fear filled my veins, and my vision flickered. My knees weakened. Nausea built up. Kids were never in my plans. I love my nieces to pieces. I'd take a bullet for them. I'd even change a shit-filled diaper. But I never wanted kids of my own.

Which is why I had a vasectomy several years ago and had followed up religiously every three months to make sure something like this didn't happen.

My fear turned into anger, and I crossed my arms against my chest. I glared at the woman sitting on my front stoop. A woman whom I had deeply cared for, hell—maybe even loved—not so long ago. But her complete and utter betrayal of my family changed that.

"You're a fucking liar, Tracie," I growled.

Her normally voluminous blond hair was tangled and matted, and it looked pathetic when she shook her head vigorously. "I swear I'm not lying. I took a test two weeks ago, but I just got it confirmed by a doctor today."

I stepped forward, getting into her space. "I haven't fucked you in over two months." Two months since the day I discovered she sold out my family to a drug syndicate, letting them kidnap and torture my sister and one of my best friends.

Her eyes widened and she stood up, lifting her chin in a bravado that was as fake as her hair color. "Which is why I'm eight weeks along. Why *we* are eight weeks along."

I chuckled darkly. "We aren't anything, Tracie. And we sure as hell not pregnant."

She shoved a paper in my face. "The test says otherwise."

I snatched it out of her hand and read it. My stomach briefly dropped at the word. Positive.

There's no fucking way. I glowered. "Oh, you may be knocked up, but it sure as fuck isn't my kid."

Tracie's blue eyes filled with tears, and she shook her head in denial. "Of course it's your baby. Despite everything that happened, this is something we created. A product of our love."

"Are you doing drugs? Our love? Did you really fucking say that?" I couldn't figure out if I should laugh or yell. The sheer audacity of this woman was insane. I ran my hands through my hair and pulled at the tips. "There is no love, Tracie. That love went away when you didn't tell me the Syndicate and the Cruz Cartel took your mom. And you made damn sure there was no love left when you tracked Charlie and Sketch's location, which led to the Syndicate torturing them!"

"I know. I fucked up. I'm sorry and I'll continue to apologize for the rest of my life. But we need to move past that. You could have let me die that night, Cole. But you didn't, and I think you know as well as I do that you still love me."

My mouth dropped open. "Seriously? In what world do you think I would take you back? I let you live because I had a moment of compassion. But believe me, had I known this shit would be going down, I would have made damn sure a bullet made it between your eyes."

"Cole!"

I rubbed the back of my neck and rolled my eyes. "Did you honestly think you could come around after everything you did? Did you think that we could forgive you? You're damn lucky Sketch isn't here, or you wouldn't be standing."

"But... I'm the mother of your baby..." she stammered.

I leaned in, coming in close to her face. "No, you're not, and you never were going to be. I can't have kids. I had a vasectomy five years ago and I go in for regular checks to make sure I don't have any active swimmers." I smirked. "In fact, I had everything checked two months ago, two days before everything went to hell. There's no way you're carrying my baby."

Realization washed over her face, and her body sagged. "You're lying," she said weakly.

"No. I'm not. I did it specifically for this purpose. I didn't want to be saddled with some crazy ass chick who thought she could baby trap me." I grabbed her arm and pulled her away from my front door, dragging her back to her Camaro. "If you truly are pregnant, I'll get a paternity test as soon as we can.

And if all odds are beaten and that kid is mine, I'll provide financially. But get this through your damn head now. I will never be with you. You got your mom back. You are alive. Take it as a win. But in the words of TSwift, we're never ever getting back together. Now get the fuck out of here before I do what I should have done last month and put a bullet through your toxic heart."

I ignored her shrieks and wails and stalked back to the house, slamming the door, and locking it. Of all the bullshit to come at me with. Never had I been so grateful to have a needle shoved through my cock than I was right at that moment.

I tossed my bag down next to the hall closet and ran my hands across my face. Seeing Tracie after being on the road for the last three weeks exhausted me more than driving an eighteen-wheeler across the country.

I made my way across the open living room into the kitchen and opened the fridge to survey my options. Unfortunately, the grocery fairy failed yet again and unless I wanted a condiment-based soup, it looked like delivery would be my only option. I pulled up the delivery app and placed an order for pizza, garlic knots, and beer, then headed for the shower. I shrugged off my clothes, leaving them in a pile for another day, and turned on the water to the hottest temp. I stood there, motionless under the rainfall while the heat pulled the tension out of my muscles.

Unfortunately, it didn't untwist my mind. My brain and gut were in conflict. The fury I had for her waged war with my conscience. I wanted to end her life, to destroy her like she tried to destroy my family.

Love. *Shit. Did I love her?* Maybe I thought I did, at the time. I know I cared deeply for her. I let her in. I trusted her. I spent more time with her than I had with anyone else. Maybe that gave her mixed signals, but I always made it clear what we had wouldn't end up with a wedding ring. The feeling I used to have for Tracie wasn't the soul encompassing love I would have wanted with a wife. I enjoyed our time together, but it felt like I had settled. It wasn't exciting and thrilling and powerful. I knew what true love felt like and this wasn't it. I gave my heart away a long time ago, and she tore it to pieces. I would never let someone have that power over me again.

Now? Fuck that bitch and the whore she came from.

I washed off the sweat and grime from the road, then got out. I had a towel wrapped around my waist and had opened the ensuite door when a loud thud came from inside of the house.

Fuck. The last thing I wanted to deal with was an intruder while my junk was flying in the breeze, so I quickly pulled on a pair of black sweatpants and palmed my Glock. If Tracie had made it past my door, I wasn't going to hold back. I flicked off the safety and crept out of my room.

Only to relax once I heard the familiar jingle of my dog's tags. I put the safety back on and stomped into the living room.

"You two are going to put me in jail or an early grave," I growled, placing the gun on the console table. My two sisters were camped out on my large, dark gray sectional, with my pizza order on the coffee table in front of them. They ignored me and continued to shove pizza in their mouths. Jax, my brindle pit bull mix came running over, his big body wiggling in happiness.

"How's it going, buddy? Did you miss me?" I crooned, my fingers scratching him behind his ears. His heavy body leaned into me, enjoying the attention. I patted his side then stood up.

"That's my dinner, you fucking heathens." I grabbed the box and settled into the far corner of the couch. Charlie, my youngest sister, gave me a look of innocence, her green eyes wide.

"We're hungry too, dammit," she groused. She wiped her mouth with a napkin and threw Jax the last bite of crust.

"Plus, think of it as payment for taking out the trash," Kate replied, her eyes not straying from her phone.

"If you mean Tracie, I sent her on her merry way once I got home." I folded the slice of NY style pizza and took a large bite. Spicy marinara tingled my taste buds and I groaned. No matter where I went, I had yet to find a pizza as good as Joe's.

Kate scoffed, her blue eyes finally catching mine. "You obviously underestimated her. After your little showdown, she stuck around. She tried to get in, but we got here before that."

"How the hell did you know I was home?"

"Zeke hacked into your doorbell camera when you went all ghost-like. We were in the area when it alerted us she was here. You happened to pull up before we made it."

"Fucking Zeke," I groaned. My teammate had more time than sense if he was hacking into my doorbell camera.

"Don't worry. We made sure to change the password for you," Charlie said gleefully.

I rolled my eyes. "I'm afraid to ask," I replied wearily.

"PurpleSparklePrincess." Kate smirked.

"Because that's manly," I grumbled, shaking my head.

"Thank your nieces for that. They were very helpful. Plus, they missed you," Charlie said with a smile.

"They really miss playing dress up with you, and making you wear the wings and crown," Kate added with a grin.

"Of course they did. I rock those wings." I cracked open a beer and surveyed the table. "You brats are buying me more pizza. And I want wings too."

Charlie rolled her eyes. "Whatever. We were hungry and you can't deny a pregnant woman food."

"The fuck I can't." I grabbed the last slice of pizza. "If you were any other chick, maybe. But you're not a random woman. You're my pain-in-the-ass baby sister. "

"Your sister that's carrying your nephew or niece, fucker!" She tried to grab the pizza, but I used my height to my advantage and held it over my head. She punched me in the gut, and I almost dropped it. For such a short shit, she had some strength behind her.

"You're mean when you're knocked up. Where's your man? Go make him buy you food," I grumbled, surrendering the last slice.

Charlie chewed the slice happily. "He's on his way to get me. We were honestly on our way to meet him at the new taco place off Waugh Chapel when we saw the toxic bitch show up."

"Well, I appreciate you running her off, but I'm good."

"We wanted to see for ourselves. We missed you," Kate said simply.

"It's not like I was gone for months. I was only gone for a few weeks," I muttered, toying with the wrapper on my beer. "Are you ordering me more food or what? I'm still hungry."

Charlie pulled out her phone and opened the app. "Yes dammit, I'm ordering your wings. I'm also including an order of those totchos."

"I don't care, just as long as you're paying." I paused, thinking of Joe's famous tater-tot nachos. "Add pulled pork and pickled jalapeños to the totchos and I'll forgive you."

She tossed her phone next to her. "Done. It'll be here in a few." She smirked. I narrowed my eyes at my little sister. I trusted her with my life, but she was a sneaky little shit.

"Good. And seriously. I told you I'm good. Me and Sketch went down to Mexico to help out his buddy, Jonesy."

Charlie narrowed her eyes. "Yeah, but Sketch came home two weeks ago, and you did not. Where the hell were you?"

"Jonesy had me haul the truck from the border to Denver, then to Florida, then finally made it home."

"Were you running women or product?" she inquired.

"Damn, nosy Rosie. What's up with the twenty-some-odd questions?" I scowled playfully. I knew she hated being the only person not in the know about missions, but it was for her own protection.

"Because this one won't tell me anything and I need something to occupy my brain now that I'm not working. So fucking give me something," she muttered, nudging Kate with her shoulder.

"Sheesh. There's a reason why, shortcake. It's classified and a need to know. You don't need to know," Kate replied, rolling her eyes.

"Pregnancy is making you cranky, shortcake." I laughed. I lift my chin to Kate. "You're awfully quiet."

"Yeah, I know. It's been a lot. Between you & Sketch running off, getting everything together for the wedding next weekend, plus Aubrey is cutting her two-year molars, and other work activities, it's been draining." She took a large bite of her pizza.

"How's the wedding plans coming along?" I was desperate for any sort of subject change and even ventured into the realm where I had no dog in the fight.

"So far so good. You got yourself situated?" Kate asked, drawing a long swig of her beer.

"Yep. Got officially internet ordained the other day. Even got the whole speech prepared." Never thought I'd get myself ordained over the internet while sitting at a truck stop, but my life had seen weirder shit.

Kate groaned and buried her head in her hands. "Don't make me regret this."

I snorted. "For someone who wants a low-key wedding, you sure are stressing."

"It is low-key, but there are still a lot of little details to figure out. The caterers, rentals, and everything else. It'll eventually fall into place. We just have to get through the next week and we'll be good."

"I got you, kid. And I promise, I won't let the strippers have too much fun with Noah at his bachelor party this weekend," I joked, and she slugged my arm. I knew my sister didn't really care if we hired strippers for my future-brother-in-law's weekend of freedom. Which is disappointing because Noah shot down my request. I guessed having a shootout at a sex club earlier this year kind of damped any sort of excitement for it. But we were still going to make the most of the evening.

My phone dinged and I quickly took a peek. "Charlie, why did I get charged for a second order at Joe's Pizza?"

"Are you sure it's not for your original order?" Charlie muttered, suddenly flustered. "Oh sorry, Sketch is on the phone." She held up the phone to her ear and stood up. "Hi babe..."

Just then, the door opened and the man in question walked in. The tall, tattooed motherfucker with the dead-gray eyes came over my sister and wrapped his tree-trunk size arms around her tiny frame.

"Ready to go, Angel?" He pressed his lips to the top of her strawberry blonde hair. He turned his gaze to me, "Welcome back. Hotwash at seven?"

I grunted and gave him the finger. I wanted to sleep in and waking up at the ass crack of dawn wasn't in my plans.

"Yep! Ready to go. Let's go. I'm ready." She quickly untangled herself and practically dragged him toward the door.

"Charlie, why are you running away so fast? Don't you want all the food you ordered?" I called out.

Sketch looked at me with narrowed eyes. "What's going on?"

I ignored his glare and replied without any regard to my safety or wellbeing. "She just bought me seventy-five dollars' worth of food from Joe's. With my own money," I replied.

Sketch scowled and pulled out his wallet. He threw five twenty-dollar bills on the table. "Don't be a dick and leave my woman alone."

"That woman is my sister. Being picked on is automatic," I snorted, pocketing the money. "Hey thanks for dinner by the way."

Charlie tucked herself in at Sketch's side and gave me the finger. "You're welcome. Enjoy the anchovies!" Cackling, she led Sketch out the door.

"She's a moody brat when she's pregnant," I grumbled. Jax's big body jumped onto the sofa next to me and nudged me with his snoot. "I don't have anything left, you big fiend. Go yell at Kate and Charlie."

Kate untangled her legs and stood up. "I better get going too. Aubrey is with Mom, so I have a rare night to myself."

"Is Noah traveling this week?" I asked.

"Yeah. He's down in Norfolk today, meeting with some potential recruits. But he'll be back in time for your after-action report tomorrow." She looked at me with a narrowed gaze. I snorted in annoyance. Just because I often slacked on doing my write ups didn't mean I wouldn't eventually get them done.

"And he'll get it. There's a lot to unpack, but I've got a good portion of it done already. The Department of Transportation only allows rig drivers to be on the road for ten hours, so I had some downtime in between stops."

"I'm sure you made great use of your downtime." She smirked. I stood up, and bent my six-three frame to hug her.

"Love you, dork. Don't worry about Saturday. I got you."

"Love you too. And I know you do. Or else I'm going to kick your ass." She grabbed her keys and phone off the table and made her way to the door, opening it as the guy from Joe's Pizza was about to knock.

"Perfect timing. There's your man. And don't forget the tip, Cole!" she joked and high-tailed it down the sidewalk.

"Did they include the tip?" I demanded. The kid's eyes widened.

"Uh... No?" he answered meekly. His ears turned as red as his hair. *Of course she didn't.*

"Fucking hell, Charlie," I groused, pulling out my wallet and shoving a twenty in the guy's hand. I yanked my food out of his hands.

I loved my sisters, but sometimes we were too damn close. And now with my two best friends being wifed up with my sisters, I didn't get any sort of space.

That's what happened when your chosen family mingled well with the family you grew up with. While it hasn't always been easy, our families blended together pretty seamlessly. Our dad was a widowed dock foreman with two small kids when he met Kate's mom at the diner where she waitressed. We ate there so frequently, Kate ended up eating with us. One thing led to another, and Kate and her mom moved into our small three-bedroom Cape Cod in Essex.

Our found family was even more intertwined. Sketch Davis, Noah Russo, and I all were in the military together, running covert operations in the nastiest of places. Kate was an agent with the FBI working undercover in Miami when she met Noah. Unknowing they were working against the same cartel target, they got together. Things got a bit messy when she realized Noah was part of our Tactical Redemption Team, but they worked it out. Noah, coincidentally, grew up close to Sketch. Noah is the father of Aubrey, whose birth mother is Sketch's late sister Jennie. We lost Jennie to the Syndicate last year, when they were plying her with so many drugs, she couldn't even register when Sebastian Cruz shot her in the head. And my sister ended up taming the cold-hearted killer beast that was Sketch.

We were a team. While normally workplace relations were typically frowned upon, the team was stronger for it. Because we weren't only an undercover black ops unit called Tactical Redemption, we were also family. You had to be when you're chasing down the worst of the worse.

After being on the road for so long, I felt restless. But the idea of getting up and going somewhere lacked appeal. I cleaned up dinner and fed Jax, then scrolled through my phone, trying to find something or someone to do. There were options, but nothing felt right.

I briefly paused on the name of someone I hadn't heard from in almost ten years. Someone who ghosted me after over a week of pure bliss. hit the dial button and lifted the phone to my ear.

"We're sorry, you've reached a number that has been disconnected or is no longer in service ..."

I jabbed the end button with my middle finger and tossed the phone onto the coffee table. Not that I expected anything different. I felt like a damn fool for trying. I wasn't sure why I still had her number in my phone. After she left me on that beach in Mexico, I had to go to great lengths to even find her house, let alone beg her grandmother to give me her phone number. I never got a chance to talk to her, because the moment I got her number, it was no longer in service. But it didn't stop me from trying it. Even while I was with Tracie, I couldn't stop thinking of Evie. One would think after ten years of silence, I would have moved on.

But I guess I couldn't. Not while my wife held my heart hostage.

TWO

Evie

I MAY HAVE BEEN the manager of this dive, but I sure as hell didn't pay myself enough to deal with horny old men.

"Don't you think you deserve a break, little lady?" If the words didn't get me hot, the slurring of his drunk, smoke-a-pack a day voice should have, right? I rolled my eyes and refilled his glass with a bottle of the watered-down whiskey I kept aside only for him.

"I just got here, Eugene. I don't need a break yet." I put the glass in front of him and set down a bowl of his favorite pistachios. The old man may have been a sleazy horn-ball, but he was also the best tipper. "Plus, you're not exactly in my age-bracket."

"I got a bottle of blue pills that will tell you that age doesn't matter." His bushy black eyebrows wiggled like caterpillars dancing. It would be amusing if it wasn't so gross.

"Let me put this plainly, Eugene. I wouldn't fuck you, even

with all the little blue pills in the world. Now finish your drink. Lucy is on her way to get you soon." I tapped the aged, dark wooden bar with my knuckles and gave him a knowing look. Lucy was Eugune's granddaughter who worked at the laundromat in the next town over. We couldn't figure out how he got here, but we had Lucy's number on speed dial and she was his taxi home, whether he wanted to leave or not.

"What the hell did you call her for? I ain't doing nothing," he grumbled and took another swig of his drink. I rolled my eyes and raised my hand to catch my barback slash day-time bouncer's attention.

"What's up, Ma?" Ivan asked as he ambled over. I rolled my eyes and smiled. These boys may be a whole foot taller than my five-three something, but they've taken to calling me ma since I was almost decade older.

"Can you please watch over Eugene for me while I go down to the cellar to stock up?" It wasn't that I thought Eugene could hop over the bar and help himself to the bottles or that he would start a fight. It was more so he could stay upright and not fall off the barstool.

"Sure thing." With an easy grin, he sat himself next to Eugune, where I anticipated he'd stay until Lucy came to pick up her granddad. Eugene had been there since at least the lunch rush, so he was more than a little sauced as we were coming into the dinner hour.

I smiled at Ivan and pushed my way into the back room. In the old building, the back room meant a series of narrow hallways and a set of steep stairs to a dark stone basement, where the underground area spanned the whole block. Beneath our bar was a series of secret passageways leading between the shops on the block. It was a maze of hidden rooms and dead ends, and perfect during the Prohibition era, where bootleggers would store their hooch or move it between shops without the

Pinkertons finding out. Each shop had its own cellar, a room dedicated to each owner. That's where we stored our alcohol. I pushed open the old wooden door, only to almost trip over a box of car parts.

"God damnnit, Dmitri." I shoved the box over with my leg and stomped over to the steel door that led to another shop.

"Dmitri! Come get your shit out of the hallway or I'm going to dump it!" I shouted, as I pounded on the door. Fucking bastard thinks that just because he owns the entire fucking block that he gets to store his car parts wherever the hell he wants.

The door creaked open and Dmitri, a portly older man with cold blue eyes stepped out. "Dorogoy, why are you so angry?"

"Because I almost tripped over your shit," I fumed. Bastard thought that calling me a sweetheart, I wouldn't bitch about his crap taking over my space. I turned back around and gestured to the multiple boxes that littered the hallway between our cellars. "Keep your car parts and rims over on your side of the room."

"You forget your place, querida. The whole building is my side." My body froze at the Spanish endearment for dear. A larger man, with a tattooed bald head and arms as big as tree trunks stepped out from behind Dmitri. Sebastian Cruz smirked and leaned against the door frame, completely blocking Dmitri from view. Knowing him, Dmitri probably went back to surveying the accounting books for their custom car parts.

Fuck. I should have known Sebastian was visiting today. He had been there at least once a week for the last four weeks. He was a dangerous snake, one who needed to be avoided at all costs. My husband, Maks, didn't fear many people, but he was surely afraid of Sebastian.

"Yes, but I can't store the products the bar needs if all your parts are mixed in with mine. Products that your clients prefer." The urge to roll my eyes was almost overwhelming but I refrained. Sebastian was a powder keg and could explode at any moment. I particularly liked my life as it currently was. Like above ground. Sebastian didn't take too kindly to any sort of implied insubordination, and especially not from females.

"I suppose I could assist." Sebastian smirked. He snapped his fingers and stepped forward, with Dmitri on his heels. Sebastain pointed to the boxes of car parts blocking my entrance into our storage room.

"Guarda estas cajas antes de que te explote los sesos." Hearing Sebastain calmly order Dmitri to put away the boxes before he blew his brain out in his native tongue should have, in a normal world, had me frozen in fear. But I'd lived this life for so long, it sounded like a normal conversation. I nodded my thanks as Dmitri struggled to move the boxes, while Sebastian stared at me. Not like a creeper, but as a predator would to his prey.

"See, I can be amenable. And now I have work I need you to do," he replied, as he followed me into the storage room. I kept my distance as I looked for the bottles I needed, but I didn't dare turn my back to him. I'm foolish, but not stupid.

I inwardly groaned. I knew it was coming. The requests weren't really requests, but orders. Ultimatums, really. Whatever he would say always came with deadly consequences if not followed. I looked at him and waited for him to continue.

"We have orders coming in." His dark brown eyes twinkled brightly at the thought. I only wanted to contribute the bare minimum to the family business, preferring to stay in my own lane and pretending ignorance is bliss. But my language skills caught Sebastian's eye, and they had other plans in mind. My participation was mandatory and he held it over my head.

I met his gaze, my spine steeled for the confrontation that awaited me. "When?"

"Next Tuesday." Sebastian grinned widely, with his teeth bared.

"We have a beer delivery coming Tuesday," I replied automatically, as I furrowed my brow in thought. As if it was a problem. It was. But not in the way Sebastian thought.

"Change it." The order was quiet but direct. A demand to be obeyed.

"I'll try. It's our normal delivery day when we get our pre-scheduled orders in." I bit the corner of my lip in concentration, as if this was something I needed to think about.

"Change. It." Sebastian's voice deepened with frustration, and I knew I was at the point that I needed to let go.

"I'll see what I can do. What sort of delivery are we expecting?" I remarked casually, but my mind raced with everything I would need to do prior to the delivery. And the timing was off. I was leaving late tomorrow night to go to Nashville with my best friend for our annual best friend vacation and didn't plan to return until Monday evening. I refused to make changes to my vacation. I was barely ever able to get away from the bar—and frankly this life—very often so I made sure that I did everything in my power to make it happen. If that included appeasing Sebastian Cruz, and the rest of the family, so be it.

"We're expecting a better batch of product, in addition to newer items that just launched. They'll need your expertise in quality control before making it to the sales floor. There are new customers in the book, along with our regulars who have reached out with some special requests." The evil spilled from his lips as he grinned. My stomach dropped and I wanted to throw up as I deciphered his orders. Sebastian always spoke in code, never trusting anyone. "Make sure you inform all customers that effectively immediately, prices have gone up twenty percent, but they'll understand why when they come to the auction."

But I kept my mouth shut and accepted the stack of papers he offered. He gave me a pointed, lingering glare as he pushed away from the door and went back over to the BCBG custom shop on the other side of the hallway.

My knees buckled and for the briefest moment, I wanted to scream in frustration. In agony for what I was going to have to do. But my back straightened, and I put the wall up around my soul. There was only so much I could do, and unfortunately, this wasn't something I could help with.

I grabbed the bottles I needed; the total number long forgotten. I hoped whatever I grabbed would be sufficient. I made my way up the creaking stairs and through the kitchen.

"Mantén la cabeza gacha y la boca cerrada," Rocco, Sebastian's cousin, muttered from his place in front of the grill, as he flipped the burgers. I sighed. Of everyone in the "family" Rocco was the kindest. His heart wasn't meant for the evils that came with being here. He didn't condone or agree with much of what Sebastian or Dmitri did or said, but like me, there wasn't much we could do.

"I know. I'll keep my head down and mouth closed," I repeated with a fake smile. He gestured to the grill with his spatula and raised his eyebrow. My stomach was too nauseous to think about eating, so I shook my head and went out to the bar area.

Looking around, I noticed Eugene had left, and Ivan had taken his place at the doorway. More regulars were filtering in. It was six in the evening, and our normal dinner rush was beginning to take shape. I hurried over to the bar where the familiar faces of this blue-collar mountain town waited.

"Ivan, take over for me. I need to go do some paperwork," I called out. I didn't wait for Ivan's lanky frame to get behind the bar, and I detoured back down the hallway. The back office was basically a broom closet with a filing cabinet, a small desk, and shit-ton of paper products like toilet paper, cleaning supplies and the like. I sat down at the black metal desk and fired up the bar's laptop. Once my VPN and connection was secure, I logged into the encrypted network and started reaching out to the twenty customers Sebastian had passed to me. I waded through my message, sending out wire instructions, along with the generic product details I had with a deadline of Sunday evening. Once the messages were sent, I turned off my laptop and slammed the lid in disgust. I grabbed the hidden bottle of bourbon in my desk drawer, the Blue Johnny Walker, and took a shot. The fire burned down my throat but I deserved the pain. I needed something to cleanse the ick from my soul, even though I knew it was fruitless.

The next three hours flew by. Between manning the bar, putting in the orders for the tables, and running interference with some of the regulars, it was a typical Wednesday night. By the time the bar started to empty out, it was last call. Once I rang the bell, the bar was left with our stragglers.

"All right boys, time to call it a night." I had already finished back-stocking the bar and set out the clean glasses Jimmy brought out from the kitchen. "Five, ten, fifteen, twen-ty." I counted the five dollar bills in my head, setting aside the piles on the bar top once I reached one hundred dollars. The regulars grumbled at my announcement.

"I don't care where you go, fellas, but you can't stay here. Don't worry, you can come back tomorrow at lunch. I hear Rocco is smoking again, so pulled pork will be on the menu," I teased with a fake smile, as Ivan and Tyler Locker, the other bar-back and bouncer, herded the rest of the stragglers out the front door.

"Good to go boss?" Ivan asked, coming back up from the

cellar. He wiped his hand on his dark blue jeans, his pale blue eyes focused on his phone. Ivan was Mak's brother, and he took his job as head of security very seriously.

"Yeah, I just need to put this back into the office." I slid the envelope holding tonight's deposit and receipts into the folder holding the paperwork I had been going through during the slow lulls and carried it into the office, where I finished up in the office and locked up. I then checked the kitchen, grabbed the dinner Rocco had set aside for me and hit the alarm. Knowing Ivan and Tyler had already done a security sweep; I followed them out and locked the front door.

"Are you in for the night, boss?" Tyler asked, his meaty hands tucked into his jeans. His dark hair fell over his eyes and for the briefest of brief moments, I could almost see him. The man that held my heart. But it wasn't him.

I gave him a fake smirk. "Nope. I got a hot and sexy date tonight. Me and my pillow are going to be sleeping together and it's going to be a threesome with my blanket. And maybe I'll even get it super spicy and bring my book with me." I grinned at the look of confusion on the two men's faces. "I've got loads of laundry to do to pack for tomorrow. Don't worry guys. My days of wilding it out on the club scene have long been over."

They laughed with me as they walked me over to my late model SUV and held the door while I got in. Their security requirement only extended to the bar, after that I was on my own. Which I was grateful for. The guys were good guys. A bit on the immature side, but they seemed to have not inhaled the Syndicate's Kool-Aid. Yet.

"I can't imagine Maks letting his woman go out on the dance floor, let alone letting her go to Nashville with her girls," Tyler remarked to Ivan, as he closed the door.

I held my tongue and grinned tightly as I waved goodbye. I

put the SUV in drive and pulled away, my façade falling quickly as I made my way down the street. Being in the middle of nowhere meant traffic on a Wednesday night was non-existent, and even less at midnight. My mind raced through the list of to-dos I had, aside from the real loads of laundry that were sitting in front of the washing machine.

After ten minutes, I finally pulled into the garage of my nineteen-seventies one level home on the other side of town and made my way inside. Only to be greeted by yells and demands from my roommate.

"Well hello to you, Mario." I rolled my eyes at the black and white cat who ruled my house. His demands for treats and dinner before I had the sheer audacity to put my stuff down was a bit much. I dropped my bag and jacket on the bench by the door and picked up the mustached feline. He protested my snuggles but I refused to let him down.

"If I'm giving you treats and dinners, I want my snuggle payment in full," I murmured against his furry head. Mario let out another pathetic whine of protest, and I acquiesced the little dictator. "Fine, you bazillion toed grump. Let's get you dinner."

The universal cat distribution system determined that I needed a furry feline friend, two months after Maks was killed. He turned up outside the bar on a rainy day, demanded his share of the smoked turkey Rocco had on the pit, and had been my constant companion ever since.

I fixed the boss his usual cup of chopped canned grossness, then ate my own dinner. Rocco made me a plate of chicken tenders and french fries, with his homemade honey mustard. The only way I didn't starve was because of him. I paid the fry tax to Mario, then walked down the hallway to my bedroom, and into the bathroom. I turned on the pipes to as hot as my water heater could go, put my hair in a cap, and climbed in. I let the hot water wash over me and hoped that it would make a difference. But even using my favorite orange-vanilla body wash didn't help relieve any tension.

I never thought I would be operating a bar in the middle of nowhere Virginia or being the wife of a Bratva enforcer. Much less a Broker for a global crime syndicate. Yet here I was. Before I learned the true ways of my family, I wanted to be a marine biologist. Spending the summers with my abuela in Sayulita, Mexico, had me spending all my time in the water. Whales and sharks were my passion, and I wanted to study them, and eventually work with them. But my life was never meant to be mine.

I was born and raised in Chicago. My parents met in college and stayed in the city ever since, building their business empires, both legally and in the criminal underworld. My mother was the leader in the commercial real estate market and my father was a master in the art of finance and banking. We weren't the typical loving family, and I learned from an early age my parents only wanted a child to further their alliances and business dealings. Family outings weren't a thing unless they were for a business function, or they needed to cultivate the guise of the perfect family. Growing up, I didn't miss what I didn't know I needed until I was older. I was a quiet, shy, bookworm who loved reading and science, with very few friends who weren't hand-selected for me. It wasn't before long when I met Maksim. Our parents were best friends, so naturally they pushed us together, to the point I was known as the tag-along to Maks and his group of friends.

I didn't know all the details of my parents' lives, but I knew I was raised differently than the rest of the kids in school. To me, having nannies, bodyguards, and guns in the house was completely normal. I thought it was completely normal for people to come in and out of the house all night, sometimes bloodied. Funerals were just as common as birthday parties, which didn't say much because I didn't attend a lot of those. I knew my family had morally gray interests, but it didn't hit me until the year I turned eighteen, when my mother died of cancer. I didn't realized how much she protected me from the true depraved horrors our families were attached to, despite never being around. Thankfully, my dad's mother insisted I spend summers with her so I could actually have a semblance of a normal life. Not only the life of the daughter of money launderers and organized crime members. But my destiny and fate were always set in stone. My life wasn't my own. All decisions regarding my future were made for me and I knew my role. I was the dutiful introvert of a daughter, who was able to be molded into the typical soldier's wife. My virginity, my purity, and my silence were my main primary attributes.

After my mom's passing, all bets were off. My role in the family became even clearer. I always knew in order to cultivate a better alliance with the Alexeyeves, me and Maks were going to marry. Even if we weren't in love, I would have to do my part to help the family. Looking back on it, I should have known better, but it was something I didn't really concern myself with when I was a lonely eighteen-year-old. I was so desperate for attention and affection I willingly took the toxic attention of a rising gangster. My father's push for the alliance increased tenfold. The pressure was enough to demand I marry Makism Alexeyevs by the end of the summer. Deep down, I wanted to speak out and stand up for myself. But I couldn't find the nerve. My father was the only parent I had left. I desperately wanted the love of family, and I lost myself in the process. The wedding date was set.

That summer, I got married. To someone else. We made our vows to each other in a Spanish Church in Sayulita, Mexico on the night of the hurricane. We whispered words of love and devotion while the candle lights flickered against the shadows of the church pews. We sought forever in each other's arms while hurricane force winds pounded on the heavy wooden door.

That night, I learned what true love felt like. It was natural, easy. Something wild and crazy but felt so right. It wasn't something you had to force or manipulate. I found happiness in the darkness and wilds of the hurricane. It was all consuming and encompassing. It was the thrill of danger, and the comfort of hearing my lover's heartbeat. It was his brown eyes that saw deep into my soul. My rebellion, my salvation.

But when the storm clouds rolled out and the morning came, I knew our two-week long whirlwind had to come to an end. I was to be Maks's. There was no future I could see where we could be happy together. My obligation was to my family, first and foremost. My golden retriever GI and I could never be free enough to love fully.

I let him go. I told him so many broken truths and lies. I broke his heart. I broke my own in the process. I wanted the choice of love, to give vows to someone I deemed important enough to share my heart with. But I knew I couldn't have it. Maks was a decent guy, and while I thought we'd eventually grow to love each other, I knew then it would never be the same. Not like what I had that summer.

I flew back to Chicago the same day and married Maks the following weekend in a lavish ceremony planned by the Alexeyeves. My future and life became theirs.

I didn't fulfill my dream of being a marine biologist, but I always knew it would never happen. They allowed me to take business classes at the local community college, but only because it would benefit the Bratva. Maks needed a wife, someone to help him rise the ranks. To keep him grounded and keep him in check. And I had to play the role of the traditional spouse and pretend to be ignorant of everything going around me. I learned how to lie well. My ignorance was a lie. I observed more than I let on. I paid attention to everything. Then came the summons from his Uncle Dmitri, who wanted to ensure the standup for their import/export business. Five years ago, we moved from Chicago to a small town outside Roanoke, Virginia to run their businesses. The businesses, a bar and a custom tire and rim shop, were legit. They made money from the townsfolk and the business people Dmitri brought in. Which also provided cover for the no-so-legit business. The business of moving product from the US to Canada. Our shops were a transit point where we would go over the product, ensure quality control and make sure the buyer had made the final payments before delivery. Alex

From as long as I can remember, we only dealt with guns and drugs. I was the person the customers went though. I managed the payment and delivery. At first, I could easily ignore the consequences of those shipments. The death toll of those shipments didn't touch me. Ignorance was bliss at that point. Maks was promoted as an enforcer, and I became the front face for both businesses. The Bratva left me largely alone. I did what I needed to do, but the groups gave me a wide berth. I didn't have to interact with anyone aside from Dmitri and Maks, and their small group of associates. I mostly dealt with the townsfolk, tourists, and Bratva customers who came to the bar. Maks was often gone on his trips for his uncle, so I immersed myself into reading and became active in the independent romance book community. I grew up and found myself. I found friends and began to enjoy life.

But I never stopped paying attention.

Business was seemingly going well, both of them. But last year, Dmitri brought in a new partner and the atmosphere went from bad to worse. The visitors were more terrifying than I had ever imagined, and the product was more inhumane. The

Alexeyeves Bratva had formed an alliance with the Cruz Cartel and a global organization called the Syndicate. And everything went to hell from there. The Cruz Cartel and the Syndicate were in the skin trade, and it wasn't only women. Pregnant women were held as incubators, only so the Syndicate could sell the babies to an adoption trafficking ring or for worse.

It was the first time I began to know fear. I wanted to reach out to my father, to get him to get me out. But deep down, I knew it wouldn't matter. My father didn't care. Maks was adamant we would be fine. He said we needed to go with the flow, and they would move on. He promised once he was pakhan, he would end this disgusting practice. Leaving the women in their cells and crates gutted me. I wanted to scream and take a gun to the faces of the cartel & Dmitri, but I knew I would die instantly. It wouldn't have mattered if my father was in cahoots with the pakhan. He wouldn't care if I lived or died, because my part in the arrangement had been completed. I would die and my father wouldn't blink.

My true purpose was crystal clear. If I couldn't stop them, I could try to save them. I kept my screams and fear to myself and vowed to avenge these children and women. I taught myself enough to cover my tracks, to ensure what I did couldn't be traced. I continued to bide my time. I couldn't save everyone, but I made sure it counted when I could.

It wasn't long before the Bratva life caught up with Mak. He died in a horrible accident last year, at the hands of a rival up-and-coming group. He was burned beyond recognition. That was the moment the life I had been living died. I went from being the face of the operation but being in the middle of it of the daily operations. It cost me so much. It cost me my husband. My life.

It wasn't something I was proud of doing, and I wanted to

scream from the rooftops and save as many people as I could. But I knew I could do so much more if I stayed.

After staying in the shower until the hot water ran out, I got out and got ready for bed. I rubbed in my favorite orange-blossom lotion and pulled on my favorite pajama set. I stared at myself in the mirror. At five-four, I was a solid size fourteen. I was curvy but had a bit of muscle tone thanks to carrying the boxes of alcohol from the cellar. I got my body shape and hair from my mama, a beautiful Black woman from Nambian decent. But my facial features, my honey colored eyes, high cheekbones, and gorgeous brown skin were all from my father's Afro-Mexican mother.

But the stress of everything had me looking rundown. I peered intently into the mirror and ran my fingers over the circles under my eyes. For a minute, I debated about using one of those high-end facial masks I purchased during one of my depression spirals but decided against it. I would make sure I did one before leaving for the airport tomorrow night. I went to my stylist yesterday, so my hair was done in silky waves, and I carefully wrapped it up in my scarf then bonnet, before moving into the bedroom.

As I went through the motions, I absentmindedly flicked on a button on the portable device and scanned my house for cameras and bugs. While I hadn't given the cartel or the Syndicate a reason not to trust me, I didn't want to take any chances. Once I got the green light as the all-clear, I pulled out the cell phone I had tucked away in a false drawer in my dresser and dialed the number I knew from memory.

"Smut-filled Book Club," the mechanical voice called.

"Hi there, I'd like to see if I could send a book bouquet to a friend, on Tuesday in the afternoon?"

"Sure thing. By which author?"

"Anne Rice, please. The Claiming of Sleeping Beauty in particular."

"I've pulled up your account. The books will be delivered on Tuesday to the address in your profile. Would you like anything else?" the monotone voice responded.

"Can we please add some greenery to the order? Perhaps some baby's breath?"

A pause. "Sure thing, we'll ensure everything will be taken care of. Someone will reach out to you this Saturday to confirm delivery."

"I'll be out of town this weekend; can I make sure they'll be able to reach me?

"They'll be participating in the One More Chapter Book event; you'll be able to meet them there if you're in town."

My shoulders relaxed slightly with relief. "Yes, thank you. I'll look for them on Saturday night."

And with that, I hung up the phone and a smidge of the tension left my body. The cryptic message wouldn't make sense to anyone who might have overheard it. The Smut-Filled Book Club was a legit business that sold book bouquets and would actually be attending the One More Chapter Book event me and my best friend were going to in Nashville this weekend. But the people on the other end of the call were not book sellers. They were the best covert operations team in the country. A network of ex-military ops groups and organizations who help victims of trafficking. And I'd been working with them for years.

THREE

Cole

FRIDAY MORNING CAME AROUND and I was ready. We had the hotwash yesterday and went over my last trip with Jonesy. I'm not sure where Jonesy came from, all I know is that Sketch crossed paths with him in South America while he was in the service and their special brands of psycho meshed well with each other. Jonsey was not someone I would want to cross. He was the leader of his own motorcycle crew and I knew I wouldn't make it out alive if I did. A bad motherfucker in his own right, but if you put him with Sketch, hellfire rained down. The women we brought from Mexico to Canada were part of a human trafficking ring with ties to the Syndicate and I had a feeling we would be working with him again soon.

But for now, work was done, and it was time to relax. It was the first time in a long while the team was together, and we weren't about to waste it.

"Let's go Jax!" I grabbed my bag and made my way to the door. My best bud was going to get some grandma-loving while I got to hang out with my boys in the woods of Tennessee. He ran out the door as I locked up when Sketch pulled up in Charlie's new Lexus SUV. My eyes narrowed at the sight of my baby sister sitting in the passenger seat and Murray the Mastiff's fathead, hanging out of the back seat window.

"Oh hell no. Come on!" I groaned, stomping over to the rear of the SUV. Sketch popped open the back lift door and I threw my bag inside and groaned again at the polka dot pink luggage my sister always insisted on having.

"Are you serious right now? This is supposed to be an all dicks and no chicks kind of weekend." I grumbled, letting Jax in before climbing in the back with them. The two dogs were both big as small tweens, and here I was, stuck in the back with the drool kings.

Charlie snorted. "I'm sure we could make it happen. I think Kate knows of a few folks who would be eager to join us.."

I rolled my eyes, remembering Kate's tales of her friends from Vegas. "Whatever. Just don't expect to be hanging around all weekend."

Sketch shot me a warning look that was partially scary. I may be big, but Sketch was bigger and had no mercy when it came to his baby mama. "You're a fucking idiot if you think I'm leaving my woman at home by herself without anyone else around for an entire weekend."

I scoffed. "I'm sure she'd be fine. She could hang out with Mom or Kate. You just want her with you so you can get your dick wet."

Sketch glared at me from the rearview mirror. "I sure as fuck ain't taking any chances. My Angel comes wherever I go."

"Ugh. Fine," I groused.

Charlie turned around and smacked me. Well, tried to anyway. Her arms were too short to reach.

"Don't be jealous he's getting laid, and you're stuck with the crazy bitch who wants your babies."

I shuddered at the thought. Shit. Tracie was the last person I slept with. Nope, that had to change. "All the more reason why this is a dicks no chicks weekend. I can't have my baby sister playing wingman at the clubs. Plus, I've been working, you evil sprite. Some of us have jobs, ya know."

"Cole," Sketch barked but I rolled my eyes. My sister was the biggest pain in my ass, but I loved her to death, and I was the only one who could pick on her.

"I am currently looking for a job, you hairy troll." Charlie fumed and she glared. I tried so damn hard not to laugh but couldn't help the snort that came out.

"It's okay, Angel. You have the most important job right now and it's making sure our bean is safe." Sketch murmured, bringing up their entwined hands and kissing hers softly.

"You're going to make me puke, dude. Seriously. I'm glad the rest of the team is coming. Wait. Does it mean Kate, Megan and Paige are coming too?" I ran my hand over my face. "Well, I guess it just means more ladies for me, Zeke, Trey, and Toren."

"It's a dual bachelor—bachelorette party. We'll do our separate things during the day and hang out at night. And as a head's up, Benji probably needs this as much as you do. He and Paige called it quits while you were gone. She was tired of him traveling and decided she wanted to be with the neighbor instead."

"Ouch. That fucking sucks. Paige and Benji had been together forever. They were like high school sweethearts. And now they have to go through the whole divorce bullshit? Yeah, this is why I'm never getting married."

"You weren't thinking of marrying the she-devil, were you?" Charlie questioned, as she scrolled through the playlist coming from Sketch's phone. Morgan Wallan's Whiskey Glasses came through the speakers, and it was the perfect soundtrack to the conversation. Shit, his music was the soundtrack to my love life.

"I briefly thought about it. But why ruin a good time with a piece of paper that causes nothing but agony and heartache?" I quipped bitterly.

"I dunno. I think it's more about the vows you make to each other, the commitment of forever," Charlie said softly, looking at Sketch while she did. He took his eyes off the road and kissed her hand again.

My heart clenched. What no one knows is I once made those vows of love and forever with someone. I thought I found my forever with the black haired brown eyed beauty who stole my heart and never gave it back. She broke my heart in a million pieces on a Mexican beach and it never grew back whole. It was for the better. She was probably all loved up with some rich dick who is home every day and can give her the bazillion kids she wanted.

"Nah, it's not for me. I'm too much for one lady to handle." I gave my sister my trademark smirk as I gestured down my body.

"Ah hell. We're not going to be able to live with your sufferable self, are we?" Sketch muttered, as he got onto interstate 695. After forty minutes of the dogs' nasty breath and Sketch and my sister muttering sweet nothings, we finally made it to my folk's house in Essex. I was so happy to pull up to the old Cape Cod style house.

I got out and stretched my legs. "Thank God you're little, Shortcake. My body isn't made to sit in the back." Sketch helped her down out of the SUV, and she rolled her eyes.

"I guess size matters when you're in the backseat, doesn't it." She gave me an evil grin and it took a minute before ...

"Hey! I'll have you know it's always bigger when—" I retort.

"La la la. Not interested." Charlie flounced away with her hands over her ears, with the dogs following behind her.

I moved to follow her, but Sketch put his hand on his chest to stop me. I look at him with an eyebrow raised.

"Two things. One—leave your sister alone. I know you guys give her crap, but she's in a hormonal phase right now. And she's still getting over everything that happened earlier this summer." I started to protest but he smacked my chest. "Just know, if she cries, I'm going to have to break your face." I rolled my eyes but inwardly, I was glad Charlie had someone crazy like Sketch to support her.

"And? What's the second, big man? We have a flight to catch so get it out," I said expectantly. Sketch glared at me. "Fine, I'll be nicer to my sister. But if she doesn't start shit, there won't be no shit. Got it? I'm not going to let her get away with crap just because she's your lady and she's knocked up, carrying the spawn of Satan."

Sketch's face turned into a grin that would scare the fuck out of any horror author. "Good. And two—We have a slight deviation in our plans."

"Fuck. Zeke didn't get the C4?" I whined. We had plans to shoot shit up on Zeke's sixty-acre property outside of the city. He had already collected an old truck, a toilet, a shipping container, and other random objects for us to blow up.

"No, you fuck wit. Zeke got a relay call yesterday. He's meeting his informant this weekend at some smut book convention."

My eyes lit up. "Smutty books? Oh, you mean what porn is for chicks. I could get down with that."

Sketch closed his eyes and pinched the bridge of his nose with his tattooed fingers. "I swear to the Gods, I'm going to strap you to the damn truck when we get to the compound."

I scoffed. "Oh please. You know Charlie wouldn't appreciate it. Plus, who would you have for comic relief? Toren? Shane? No way. I'm a fucking delight."

Sketch shook his head. "I'm going to need more bail money, aren't I?"

I slapped him on the back and chuckled. "Think about it. It's either money for hookers or bail. You pick." I made my way up the sidewalk, and all the while I could hear Sketch mumbling under his breath.

"I was talking about bail for myself. Not for you."

I smirked as I let myself in my house and inhaled. The scent of lemon cleaner with sugar cookies filled the air.

"Hi ma." I curled my arms around my small mom and kissed the top of her head. Charlie may not have gotten any of her genes from Cathy Parker, but they were very similar in height.

"Hi baby boy. Are you ready for your break." She smelled like cookies and... I sniffed again.

"Yeah, but are you holding out on me?" I pulled back and glared at her.

Her blue eyes, the same ones Kate inherited, narrowed, and her brows arched. "What are you implying, son of mine?"

I gently moved her aside and stalked toward the kitchen. She was hiding them from me. I knew it. I searched the oven and through the cabinets. "Where is it, mom?" I called out.

I heard her sigh from the kitchen entryway. "Where is what, Cole?"

I spun around and pointed a finger at her. "You made them. Where is the container of my cookies?"

Mom shook her head and gave me a large smile "Cole. There are no cookies. At least not now. I made them, but they were for a neighbor. I just dropped them off."

My mouth dropped in sorrow. "What? Are you serious? Tell me you're lying." Her silence told me everything. I felt so betrayed.

"What the hell is going on? Why are you in the kitchen? We need to be on the road. Toren's plane isn't going to wait forever." Charlie demanded. I glared at her. I bet mom didn't give her cookies away. We all had our own cookie flavor. Kate's was a strawberry cookie with cream cheese icing. Charlie's sweet tooth loved all kinds, but her favorite was the pumpkin chocolate chip. And then there's mine. Mom called it the trash can cookie. It was full of yummy goodness with M&Ms, pretzels, butterscotch, chocolate chips and peanut butter chips. Mom always made me a container of these when I was deployed. And to hear she shared my cookies with some stranger, I almost wanted to cry.

"Mom made my cookies and gave them to someone else." I sulked. Yes, I was a thirty-one year old man and I sulked. Because...cookies.

"For fucks sake, you're acting like a toddler. You shouldn't be going to Nashville if you're going to act like that." Mom claimed in exasperation. She went into the laundry room and brought out a container. She shoved them in my hands. "I was going to give them to the new mom who just moved in down the block but look at you sulking and having a temper tantrum over cookies. Sheesh." Mom blew a lock of her blonde hair out of her face and gave me the universal mom look of disappointment. I know I should have felt bad. And for a brief second I did.

But the guilt disappeared once I took a bite of the still

warm deliciousness. "I love you, mom." I said with my mouth full.

She rolled her eyes then wrapped her arms around my waist. "I love you too, trouble. Now get. Remember, don't get arrested and behave. Whatever happens in Nashville, never stays in Nashville."

"Let's go, fucker. Toren's already texting me to see where we're at and the airstrip is thirty minutes away." Sketch growled, as he walked in from talking with my dad outside. He gave my mom a hug and took Charlie by the hand, leading her out.

"Bye mom. Thanks for watching the dogs. We'll be back on Monday." I hurried after them and jumped into the back seat. My door was barely closed before Sketch threw the truck into drive.

"Geez, trying to kill me there, speed racer?"

"Your blabbing about cookies has us running late. Thankfully, the rest of the crew are already there." Sketch muttered. He reached behind him into my personal space and held out his hand.

I slapped it.

"No, fucker. Give me a fucking cookie or I'm tossing you out." He growled.

"Sheesh. Fine. Here." I slapped a cookie in his hand. "No more. You're lucky I'm sharing with you." I narrowed my eyes at his baby mama. "And don't even think about asking for one."

Charlie shrugged. Then she revealed her own box of cookies. "I didn't have to throw a fit for mine."

I didn't have a good comeback so I just gave her the finger and chowed down. I hadn't eaten this morning and the energy drink I had earlier was waning. I was looking forward to the weekend with the guys. Shooting the shit, blowing up stuff, just being us without having to worry about drug cartels and human trafficking. But we wouldn't truly get a break. We were always on the clock, but we left our second line of team members ready and able at Tactical Redemption. Organized crime doesn't pause for vacations or weddings.

We made it to the airstrip in less time than we thought. Toren Rodriguez, a team leader in our unit, was richer than God apparently. Not only was he a silent investor in Tactical Redemption and a former Green Beret, but he also worked in finance on the side. Doing what, I had no clue but whatever he did, he made a shit-ton of money. So when it came time to plan Noah's bachelor party, he volunteered the use of his private jet. Thankfully for us, it also could accommodate the extra stowaways.

When we finally parked, Noah and Kate were waiting for us by the entrance, along with the rest of the team. Everyone was ready for the weekend. I looked around. The ladies were in sundresses; I guess it was a bride thing. My sister in her deep rose sundress, Charlie in a light teal, and Megan in a dark navy.

"You're looking gorgeous as ever, Megs." I pulled her into my arms and laughed at Shane's glare. There may have been a time when Shane couldn't get his head out of his ass, and I almost tried to shoot my shot with the beautiful Megan. Her dark brown hair and eyes, plus her curves, could bring a man to his knees. In fact, it did. Shane was a goner ever since he met her, way back in the day after his parents passed away and his aunt took him in.

"You're still a charmer, Cole," she said with a tease, as her arms wrapped around my waist.

"Don't you know it, sweet cheeks. Have I charmed you enough to run away with me? Or are you still stuck with this doofus?" I smirked in Shane's direction. "You know, he may be your baby's dad, but I can ..."

"Go fuck yourself. That's what you can do," Shane replied dryly.

"Sorry Cole. You missed your chance. I'm kinda stuck with him now," Megan joked, pulling away.

"I mean, I didn't say you had to divorce him. I hear throuples are a thing now." I teased.

"Yeah, nah. I grew up with your dumb ass. I'm not forming a throuple with you," Shane groaned.

"Come here you big fucker. You know you love me," I said to Shane, my childhood best friend. I grabbed his hand and pulled him into one of those half-hugs. "I missed my bestie. Someone who loves me. You don't know what I had to go through on the way here. I had to deal with Sketch and the evil preggo over there, and don't get me started about mom trying to hand out my cookies."

"Get in the fucking plane, Cole." Charlie said dryly, as she climbed the staircase. Sketch was right behind her, staring at her ass.

"Dude. Not in front of her brother!" I chastised. He gave me the finger as they ducked into the cabin. "See, this is why it should have a 'no girls allowed' trip. No offense, Megs." I said quickly, hugging her again. I laughed at Shane's snarl. I loved getting him riled up. She laughed and shrugged.

"We really didn't get a bachelor/bachelorette party when we got married. So, we're excited to have this time too." She looked at Shane and nudged him. "I'm ready for the lap dances."

Shane glowered. "Unless it's a hot chick or me doing my best magic Mike impression, it ain't happening."

Megan smirked and shrugged her shoulders. "We'll see what happens when we get to Nashville." She winked and sashayed up the steps in her blue sun dress. Shane's eyes followed each step.

"You got a little drool there," I joked, gesturing to the corner of his mouth.

"You're damn straight I do. You would too if you were able to come home to this beauty every day." He turned and smacked me on the chest. "Don't worry, I promise we will get a room close to yours so you can hear what you're missing."

No thanks. The last thing I needed was thin walls and horny couples. I seriously need to get laid.

"So, you're saying I need to get some ear plugs. Great. Good idea. Or maybe I can join you," I called to his back.

"I'll sooner cut your dick off!" Shane shouted back.

I turned to Trey, Benji and Zeke and shook my head. "He didn't mean it."

"The hell I didn't!" He shot back from the inside of the plane.

"Broadway is calling for us, fellas. Let's make sure she knows our name by the end of the weekend," Trey smirked, as he grabbed my shoulders and shook them in excitement. We stumbled on board, and as soon as we were all settled in the plush, beige seats, we started pushing away from the terminal. After a few short minutes, we were airborne.

Conversations continued around me, with Trey, Benji and Zeke the most boisterous. It had been a long time since any of us were able to get away from the shop. Between the training we've been providing for the local and federal officers, and going after the Syndicate and Cruz Cartel, we've been stretched too thin. It didn't help that I was out of pocket for the last month and a half, helping Jonesy rescue his woman and her family from a trafficking ring in Mexico.

I met Sketch while in the jungles of Columbia, as our two teams met up to go after a kingpin with a penchant for small children. It wasn't too long before our roads crossed again, this time in Africa with Noah. We clicked instantly. We had each other's backs, and before long, we were brothers. After Sketch and I left the military, we joined forces to build up our business. Tactical Redemption was originally designed for tactical training and mission assistance. We were funded by Department of Defense contracts, along with local and federal law enforcement, so between that and our background in the military, we're at the top of our game.

We were originally brought in to help the feds with an up-and-coming drug cartel. The Cruz Cartel was making strides in the guns and drug trade. Which is how I finally got to catch up with Shane after years of no contact. He was a dealer for the cartel, turned federal informant. He worked with Kate and the FBI on bringing in the information to the feds. Kate knew there was an inside agent, and with Shane's help, she discovered it was a fellow FBI agent, Tommy Greene, now known as Tommy Cruz. He was the elusive son of the cartel kingpin, Christian Cruz. Then shit the fan. With Christian dead at the hands of his son, the cartel was under the control of Tommy and his two brothers, Elias, and Sebastian. The cartel had joined forces with an organized group called the Syndicate. A global alliance most organized crime families belonged to. The Russian and Belarus Bratvas, the Japanese Triad, the Costa-Nostra, and the Cruz Cartel were just a sampling of the players who were involved. Each group had their own piece of the action, and with a representative from each family on the board, there was some sort of agreement to not go after each other's turf. It was them against the world, and they have influence from within their respective governments. Corruption at its finest. You never knew who was on whose payroll. Including members from the Titan Edge team where Sketch, Noah, and I came from.

A member of the Titan's Edge team was responsible for bringing Sketch's sister Jennie to Vegas. He went from a respective team member to Sebastian Cruz's crony. I took great delight in shooting the bastard in the face.

The Syndicate had managed to fuck with pretty much everyone in my family, and I wanted nothing more than to watch them burn to ground. Charlie lost her job because the biotech company she was interning for was in bed with the Syndicate, trying to create a more addictive combination drug. Thanks to Tracie, they kidnapped Charlie and Sketch, and made Charlie create new formulas, only to test them on Sketch, who was already a recovering drug addict. They killed Jennie, Sketch's sister. They targeted my niece, Shane, and Megan as well.

Two months ago, they came to our door and tried to ambush us at Tactical Redemption. Needless to say, We began operating in the shadows. Sure, we publicly provided firearms and tactical training, but everything else? Nah, we were in the black. We were the team the feds called in when they couldn't get their hands caught in the cookie jar. We weren't on the books, and we were sure as fuck not under some government oversight. Very few people had our number, and we kept it that way for a reason. Trust was a very expensive commodity, and we didn't have much of it to give away. We were our own team, ran our own rules, and fought the fights that no one wanted to be a part of.

The two-hour flight went by quickly. Before I realized it, we landed in a private airfield outside of Nashville. Toren had arranged for two large SUVs to bring us to Zeke's compound located outside of the city. We piled in and made the thirty-minute trek, and soon we drove up the winding concrete drive-way. Situated on a secluded hilltop, the log-style mansion was surrounded by sixty acres of forest.. Zeke had purchased this home after the shit went down with Sketch and Charlie. They spent two months on the run, staying in different cities and constantly on the move. What we needed was a safe house. While we had the one in Vegas, we wanted something within a day's drive, for when the time came to bug out. So through a series of legitimate corporations and trusts so his identity couldn't be determined, he purchased this piece of seclusion.

We pulled to a stop at the front door and everyone stumbled out, in awe of the majesty surrounding us. The forest was thick and the sounds of birds were plentiful. But the best sound was the quiet from the everyday hustle and bustle. The sound of peace.

"The Cumberland River is a few minutes away, but there's a spring down toward the base of the hill. The toys are close by, we'll do all our playing about a mile east. I have a shed out there, with a fridge and outhouse. We'll just have to take the gators to it."

"Bring on the toys, man," Trey said with a crazy grin. The fucker was already bouncing on his toes, ready to get the action going.

"Let's get situated first, then we can take out the bikes. There are four dirt bikes here too, along with a golf cart, so we'll be able to cart everyone around," Zeke replied dryly as he went to unlock the door. After a series of buttons on the lock and an actual physical key, he finally opened the door. "Well. Come on and don't let the bugs in."

We trailed behind him, and the interior was just as amazing as the outside. No expense was spared, from gleaming hardwood floors to the vaulted ceilings and two-story windows. The largest couch I've ever seen sat in front of a ninety-inch projector TV, with a shelf of all the available video games underneath it. This was the ultimate man-cave.

"Let me show you around," Zeke said, dropping his keys on the counter. He led everyone through the house, pointing out the industrial kitchen, the six bedrooms with attached ensuites, and game room. The couples immediately paired off, leaving the single guys to double up on the last three bedrooms with queen beds in each room.

"This is some bullshit. I didn't come out this way to snuggle with your hairy ass," Benji grumbled, as he brought his duffle bag into the room. "What happens if I find someone to dip my dick in? Is this going to be like the barracks where I put a sock on the door?"

Trey snorted and threw a rolled-up ball of socks at Benji's head. "Don't act like you were getting pussy while in the field." I felt bad for Benji though. He had been with Paige since he was out of high school. They were married right before he deployed to Iraq, and despite all the misgivings of some people, he remained faithful to her the entire time. Unfortunately, we couldn't say the same thing about her.

Benji shook his head and looked down at the bag he was unpacking. "Yeah, well, maybe I should have been."

"Didn't they say the best way to get over a chick is to get on top of another one?" Zeke joked, coming in from the other room.

"I'm down," Benji muttered. He pulled back his light blond hair back into knot at the back of his head.

"Good. I figure we'll hit the clubs tomorrow night. I know Kate booked a spa day or some shit for the girls, so they're headed out. Why don't we go blow some shit up and then fire up the grill?" Zeke replied with a smirk. If Benji couldn't have pussy, the next best thing for our explosive expert was blowing shit up.

We followed him back to the main living area, where the pussy-whipped jerks were saying goodbye to their girls. It never failed to surprise me how different Sketch was with Charlie. On the field, he was known as a merciless killer, haunted by demons from previous battles and a rough home life. When the drugs got a hold of him, he was worse. He was numb, impervious to the daily dealings going on every day. The day I got him to the hospital after overdosing, I gave him an ultimatum. Get clean and we'll start Tactical Redemption, but I couldn't work with someone I couldn't trust around a weapon.

Thankfully, he understood. Sketch took the first step and spent three months in an in-patient rehab facility, and once he got out, went to out-patient care three times a week. He got better but the demons and monsters were still there. Until Charlie made him see the light. And while he's still the same merciless killer on the battlefield, there's more of a humanity about him now.

Zeke had thought ahead and had a taco bar catered in, so we dug in before checking out the weapons depot which was housed just a bit aways from the main house. The security on this property was beyond anything I have seen before. Between the night-time sensors, cameras in every corner and the lights, motion detectors, and stockpile of weapons, I knew where I was going if and when there was ever a zombie apocalypse.

"Oh, this is purty," I whistled as I picked up the shiny black sniper rifle. "This hasn't hit the market yet, and I know the DOD was just now building the prototype." I looked at Zeke with my eyebrow arched. "Are you building the prototype, Zeke?"

Zeke shrugged, but the man couldn't lie for shit around me. I was the human lie detector. I could smell bullshit from a mile away. I may not be the smartest man of the group, but I can read a person in no-time, just based on their body language and background.

"Yeah, well, I had to pay for the house somehow," he said sheepishly. He loaded the cases up on the four-wheeler's trailer and climbed on. "The last one to the field has to clean up the shell casings!" He called over the roar of the engine. His words died in the wind as he took off and headed east.

Fuck! No one wanted that mess. We scrambled for the remaining modes of transportation. Shane, Benji and Noah grabbed the remaining three four-wheelers, and there was only a golf cart and a gator left. I left Trey and Toren to duke it out and sprinted to the dirt bike leaning against the wall of the house. I knew I could smoke all those fools if the damn dirt bike could work. I hoped on, and thanked whoever was watching over me the keys were in the ignition. I gunned the engine and took off, only coming in third behind Noah.

"Ha! Suckers!" I crowed, as I drove past the rest of the group. I could hear Trey bitching about being in last place as I turned around. I parked the bike and slapped Zeke's hand. "Thanks for the bike, bro. I need one of those things at home."

"I didn't even see the damn thing," Trey grumbled. He looked a little put out by having to drive a golf cart, but whatever. All's fair in love and guns.

The rest of the day was the day of my dreams. We blew up an old school bus, shot up some markers, and held some good old friendly target competition. Once as the sun started to set behind the mountain, we reloaded everything and cleaned up and headed back to the house. The lights were ablaze and we knew the girls were home.

Sure enough, the three lucky bastards with ladies were greeted with kisses. I tried to get a kiss from the only female I wasn't related to, but Shane shoved me off her before I could get a good smooch. Fine. Jerk.

After we ate, we drank our body weight in Zeke's family moonshine. The shit was potent, and I was half worried someone would get alcohol poisoning. Two by two, the couples headed to bed. I could only hope the walls were thick enough to muffle any sounds. The last thing I needed to hear was sex noises when I was amid a dry spell.

I looked over the rim of my glass at the rest of the guys. "Tomorrow. It's all chicks on the dicks, boys. It's happening. I can feel it." I couldn't feel my lips, or really my tongue, but hey, I wouldn't be wrong. Tomorrow night was going to be the best time.

FOUR

Evie

"HAPPY DIRTY THIRTY, BITCH! DRINK UP!" A shot of tequila pushed my way across the glossy bar top. I arched my eyebrow at my best friend, Macie. She looked at me with an expectant grin, her eyes glassy from the previous shots of tequila. I shook my head and smiled, tapping my glass against hers and downed the sweet spicy liquid, wincing as the burn made its way down my chest. One of my favorite things about Macie is that she knows her liquor and doesn't order the cheap stuff.

"You know I'm not thirty, right? I'm turning twenty-nine," I replied with a smile, my eyebrow arched.

Macie waved her hand in dismissal. "Close enough. I couldn't think of anything that rhymed with twenty-nine."

I shrugged. That was Macie for you. She flipped her honey gold hair over her shoulders and fanned her face.

"Another one?" she asked, raising her voice over the noise surrounding us.

"Yeah, then let's go find the others." She pushed my hand away when I tried to hand over my card to the bartender.

"It's your fucking birthday. Your money is no good here." She scoffed and flashed her beautiful smile to the woman behind the bar.

"Then I got the next round," I argued, putting the card back into my front pocket. Macie rolled her eyes and tapped her new shot against mine.

"We'll see," she said with a smirk. "Now drink up."

I obliged, taking the shot. I missed this woman so much and I was so glad we managed to get away for this girls' weekend in Nashville. We were here for a large romance novel convention. After a few days of mingling with authors, it was time to unwind and have a great time. We were both huge book nerds, and we were lucky enough to meet through an online romance book club. While we were here because we were smut junkies, Macie was also here on business. Macie had her cute corner bookstore in her town and was always looking to bring more indie authors onto her shelves.

We spent the rest of the night mingling with our friends, readers, and authors at the afterparty. The stress from the day— from waiting in the lines to the crowds to the chaos— just melted away.

"I'm so glad you finally were able to come," I said warmly. She rolled her eyes and grabbed my hand. It'd had been at least four months since she was able to get away. Her business was a complete success, and it was about time she took some time for herself.

"You know I wouldn't miss your birthday and the biggest book convention of the year. But seriously. Between the shop and everything going on with Daniel's campaign, I barely had time to breathe." I internally rolled my eyes at his name. Her boyfriend, Daniel, was a source of contention between us. He was the son of a senator and had his daddy's money and mom's political influence to get whatever he wanted. According to Macie, he had his eyes on her since she moved to their small town in North Carolina. I didn't like him. He came off as the typical political asshole, completely phony and only looking out for his own self-interests. But for some reason, Macie loved him. He made her happy, so I tolerated him.

"How are you guys doing?" I asked. Daniel himself would stress anyone out. Daniel campaigning for local politics would be enough for the strongest person to scream.

"We're okay. It's just stressful. There's just a ton going on and I'm really glad I got a chance to get away though. I needed this time to just be with my bestie." She gave me my hand a squeeze, then something caught her eye. "Oh my god! There's Carrie-Ann Ryan! I want to chat with her about a signing at the shop."

"I'll catch up with you," I replied absentmindedly, taking another sip of my Cosmo. I checked my phone, but the music called my name. I stood and headed to the dance floor. My body swayed in time with the music, and I closed my eyes, losing myself in the beat. The combination of sex in the air and tequila in my had my body on fire. The deep base pulsed through and let my body move. The dance floor became heated with the crowd, and I let myself feel. Forget the drama and stress waiting for me back home. Tonight, it was about being free.

This weekend was all for me. It was my twenty-ninth birthday, and I needed to get away from all the drama. I needed a chance to live before I went back to the prison which had become my life. I was only thankful that they thought so little of me to let me travel to Nashville without question.

For the next thirty minutes or so, I danced. I danced by myself and with others. I let my body move in ways I haven't done in so long. In almost ten years.

But something made the hair on the back of my neck prickle. As if on command, I turned my head, only to lock eyes with him across the room. My heart stopped. He was tall, with a black button-down stretched across his large chest. His silky brown hair draped over his eyes, but I felt the heat of his stare, nevertheless. The familiarity of those eyes hit me in my soul. My breath hitched as he pushed off the railing he was leaning against and made his way through the crowd.

Toward me.

I felt like prey and he was the apex predator. My body continued to sway, as if I was in a trance. I wasn't a shy girl, by any means. Macie said I have confidence in spades. You would have to in my situation. Weakness was not an option. But something in this man had me tongue tied. The familiarity was striking, and I knew I knew him from somewhere. I was in a dreamlike state. So much so I startled at my best friend's voice in my ear. She laughed at my reaction and looked over her shoulder.

"Who is that?" she asked, her blue eyes wide. I shook my head to focus and suddenly, he was gone. I couldn't see him anywhere and disappointment filled me. Could it have been him? Could it have been Cole? The Cole I was married to in Mexico was smaller in stature, not as broad and sure as hell didn't have tattoos on his arms. It's not him, just someone who looked a lot like him.

I shook my head. "I don't know. But let's grab a drink." She nodded, and I led her back to the bar. I took one glance over my shoulder and the spot was once filled by the mystery man was now vacated.

I wasn't sure why disappointment filled me. It's not that I have even talked to the guy. It wasn't him. Why would I think it's him? I shook off the feeling of familiarity and made my way through the crowd, holding Macie's hand.

We settled up at the bar and I smiled at the gorgeous barkeep. "Can we please have a lemon drop martini, an old-fashioned, and two shots of tequila?" It may have seemed like a lot, but the bar was busy as hell, and we were in a time crunch.

"Where did you go? I saw you talking with Rebecca Yarros and then you disappeared."

Macie's face went blank. I knew the girl well enough to know she was lying. We've been friends since we met on a Book Club's social media group three years ago. We clicked immediately when she convinced me to read a Shantel Tessier novel. Since then, we talked every day and at least once a month, I tried to make the four-hour trek to her small town in North Carolina, where we would bond over our love for morally gray men, drink, and basically chill all weekend. While organized crime was currently my life, I couldn't help but fall hard for the dark romance baddies. There was nothing wrong with wanting a little villain action. It was my time to be myself and disassociate from the trials of being with the Syndicate.

My eyebrow arched as I waited expectantly. I may not have seen it with my own eyes, but I knew there's something more going on where she didn't want to tell me. I knew what keeping a secret looked like. I was used to keeping many from her, thanks to my questionable relationship with Maks and his friends, to what went on outside of our sleepy little town. She was innocent. Most of the people that lived near us were innocent and I sure as hell wouldn't drag her down with me.

"Had to run to the restroom." The answer was bullshit and we both knew it. She bit her lip and fiddled with her fidget ring.

Thankfully, we were interrupted by the bartender placing down the two shots and our drinks. "Cheers, bitch. Happy Birthday to me" I toasted. Macie's smile widened as she threw back the shot. I winced as the fire went down my chest. Damn that shit was good.

"You need to get laid."

I choked on the remnants of the shot at Macie's nonchalance. "Where the hell did that come from?"

"How long has it been, Evie?" She ignored my question and gave me a pointed look as I picked up my lemon drop. "How long as it been since you've been thoroughly fucked? Since your legs were jelly and aftershocks were never-ending? How long has it been since you had an orgasm?"

"Fuck, Macie." I groaned, as I took a gulp. I'm going to need more liquor to keep up the conversation. If she kept this shit up, I was going to have to order another one.

"Fuck is right. It's exactly what you need to be doing." She took another sip of her old-fashioned. "You're in Nashville, Tennessee. There has to be some cowboy you want to ride."

I quickly glanced around at the potential audience, but I knew it was hopeless. I'm sure everyone and their cat heard her. As loveable as Macie was, she had no control of her volume once tequila hit her system. A Black man, with sensual hazel eyes and a sinful body caught my eye and gave me a smirk. Yep, he heard her. I groaned.

"This isn't a conversation I'm really in the mood to have here in public." I gave her a wide-eyed glare. Of course, it set off her drunk giggles and I couldn't help but join in. My purse vibrated and my heart sunk. It was time to go.

"Let's finish these drinks and go somewhere else," I said to my bestie. I drained the rest of my glass and hopped off the barstool, the vodka already buzzing in my system. We locked hands and we made our way through the crowds. I was halfheartedly listening to Macie, but I kept my eyes peeled for my mystery man. My. He's not my anything. We finally exited the bar and made our way over to the Walk of Fame Park.

"There's this really cool light exhibit going on tonight and I want to take a look at it," I rambled, my stomach fluttering at what was about to happen. I suddenly paused and whirled around, causing Macie to bump into me.

"Evie, what's going on?" I knew she was feeling buzzed, but not totally drunk. At least not yet. Indecision flooded me, and I hoped I was doing the right thing.

"Macie, tell me the truth right this second. Are you in love with Daniel? Be one hundred percent honest with me." I demanded softly.

Her brow furrowed in confusion. "Where is this coming from? Yes, I love Daniel. We're just going through a rough time."

"Are you sure?" I insisted.

"Yes. Of course... Why? What's going on?" She moved past me to turn the corner, and gasped. I turned around and took in her surprise. Flickering candles were laid out in the shape of a heart on the ground. Daniel, dressed in a sharp black suit, was waiting in the middle, and looking at the love of his life with stars in his eyes. Macie froze, with her eyes wide in shock. I gently took her hand and led her over to Daniel. He nodded his thanks, but his eyes stayed on Macie. I stepped back and glanced to my left, grateful to see the photographer and videographer I hired capturing the moment.

I couldn't hear what Daniel was saying, but I watched as Macie covered her mouth and saw the tears running down her cheeks. Daniel got down on one knee and presented a ring to Macie, and a cheer came up from the crowd surrounding them as she nodded yes. I caught a glimpse of their parents, wiping away their own tears. Daniel was not the one I believed she was supposed to be with, but that ship had long since sailed. And while I may not be the biggest fan of Daniel, she seems happy, and she says that she loves him. That's all I cared about.

I stuck around the park with her friends and family, before giving my best friend a hug and Daniel whisked her away. We had planned this for weeks, and Daniel had a suite lined up for them. We had her bags packed and sent over to his hotel after we left for the book signing, so I knew I wouldn't see my bestie until the next time I went to North Carolina. I walked back through the park, and noticed a shadow of a man, lingering near the entrance. Any normal woman's spidey sense would be blaring right now, but I knew who it was. I had planned this meeting.

"Hello Raven," the voice said softly. I looked up at the man with incredibly beautiful dark brown skin and sinful eyes. The same man who had witnessed Maci's declaration at the bar.

"Hello Griff." I replied. He took my wrist and pulled me into the shadows. Yes, our code names were taken from Harry Potter, but when a book nerd meets a gamer nerd, it just worked.

"The shipment is coming on Tuesday?" he murmured. He wrapped his arms around me, and I could smell his delicious cologne. To the naked eye, we looked like lovers embracing. Not an informant and a covert operator talking about a human trafficking delivery.

"Yea. Looking like women and children. From the sounds of it, there could also potentially be babies as well." Bile bubbled in my stomach, and it wasn't from the alcohol.

"Fuck. Don't worry, Raven. We're on it. How are you doing? Are you ready to come in yet?" His gravelly voice sounded in my ear. His arms tightened around me, and for a moment, I felt the comfort of having someone care. It had been so long since I had been held.

"Not yet. I have to see this through." Once we brought down the transport operation, I would get out of dodge. I needed to bring down the Syndicate, and my father. Fuck. Everyone who had been involved was going down.

"You know this could backfire on you at any moment. Anytime these transports are taken, you're liable to be blamed."

I shrugged, scared but resolved. "I know. And that's a risk I'm willing to take. I'm a part of this life, Griff. This is my role to play."

Griff lowered his head, placing his forehead against mine. I could smell cinnamon and whiskey from his breath. "Just be careful, Evie. You're more important than you think."

I was a little shocked at the use of my real name. We've never addressed each other by our names, just by our code names. "Am I to call you Zeke now?"

He scoffed. "You could call me Daddy, or anything else you want, darlin,' but I think someone else would object." My eyebrows raised at the remark.

"My husband is dead, Zeke. There's no one who could object."

"Don't be too sure." I rolled my eyes at his cryptic remark. "Anyway, we're good. I'm sending someone for your regular delivery Monday afternoon, and they'll stick around for a while, at least until the cargo is secured and safe. We've got plans in place for coordinated ambushes, so the focus won't only be on this particular route."

I nodded. "Anything else?"

"Yeah, go have a good time. You deserve it." And with that, Zeke stepped further into the shadows and walked away. I stayed behind for a few minutes, to get my thoughts in gear. Zeke took a great risk in meeting me here, but my thoughts swirled around what he said about multiple transports being targeted. Could this be the beginning of the end for the Syndicate?

I shook my head to get rid of my thoughts and made my

way through the park, back to the main street. Zeke was right. I deserve a good time. I missed the warmth and feel of a man's body close to mine. I debated about going back into the club. The idea of ordering dinner in my pajamas appealed to me, but I was in Nashville on my birthday. There was no way I was going to be alone on my birthday.

The bouncer let me back in and I was enveloped by the heat. I waved to a few book friends who had stuck around and moved to the dance floor.

I couldn't lie to myself. I wanted to lay eyes on my mystery man. But as I gazed around the crowded club, I didn't see him. The potential for a one-night stand in Nashville was intriguing. Despite my protests to Macie, it had really been a long time since I had toe-curling sex. Maks was decent enough, but I was often left unsatisfied in the bedroom, unless we used toys. But since he died almost a year ago, I felt guilty looking for someone to replace him. And if I was truly honest with myself, I didn't want to subject anyone to the potential scrutiny by the Syndicate and the Bratva. But really, it was beyond that. Just once I wanted someone to care for me, to care about my needs, hopes, and dreams. Not to live my life by the order of the Syndicate and the business whims of my father.

I let myself melt on the dance floor. I let go. I let go of all the stress, the demons that haunted me, of not doing enough, of trying to be the perfect daughter and wife.

I let go.

Even though my strapless, black bodycon dress left little to the imagination, I felt confined. Restless. I needed to release whatever stress in my body. Alcohol and dancing seemed to be the only options right now.

My skin prickled before I felt his heat on my back. Inwardly I knew. I didn't have to look. He didn't grab me or press against me, but he stood close enough. His fingers gently glided down my arm, as if asking for permission to get closer. I stepped toward him, my back against his chest. A thick arm wrapped around my waist holding me against him tightly. His attraction was evident at the small of my back. I let my head fall back against his barrel chest, and he bent down, his face tucked into the crook of my neck. He audibly inhaled deeply and my core clenched.

His presence felt like a balm to my soul. I felt complete with this total stranger. My body relaxed in his embrace, and we swayed to the music, with the tickle of his facial hair against my shoulders.

"You smell delicious as you look, kitten." The low growl in his voice sent an electric shock straight to my cunt. His lips moved up my neck, sucking and nibbling lightly as he went. One hand traced a path from my stomach to the hem of my dress. I whimpered and squeezed my thighs together, as he stoked the fire in my veins. The other hand reached up to cup my neck, gently squeezing to test my preference. The pressure on my throat was tight enough to where he could feel me swallow my moan. I responded by grinding my ass into his pelvis, where his thick cock pressed against me.

He growled, low and deep. "Kitten, I'm trying to take this slow, but if you don't behave, I'm going end up fucking you on this floor in front of everyone."

I couldn't help it when a moan escaped. My panties were soaked. I rubbed my thighs for some relief, but of course it didn't work. Mystery man chuckled darkly, his voice low in my ear. "Maybe that's what my kitten wants. To be thoroughly fucked in front of all these people." I gripped his hand and pushed it under my skirt, to where I needed him the most. He groaned as he traced the edge of the wet lace. The dance floor was packed but I didn't care. I needed him inside me, like I needed my next breath.

He toyed with the lace, his finger sliding over my slick lips.

"I don't want my first taste of you in forever to be in the middle of a fucking crowd, kitten. I'm in the hotel next door. Meet me at the penthouse. Ten minutes, Evie." My pussy clenched and my breath quickened as a cool draft against my back. He disappeared but the air helped to clear the haze of lust. He knew who I was. Just as I knew who he was.

Cole.

Underneath the bullshit, I knew it was him. My soul sang for his. After all this time, the sound of his voice had me in a puddle. I needed him. I needed to be with him. Even though I knew it would end badly, I needed to go.

I hurried to the bar and ordered a shot of tequila. A shot of courage was necessary. I didn't know how it would go. I hadn't seen or heard from Cole in almost ten years. The bartender poured a hefty shot and slid it over. I threw it back and laid a twenty across the counter. My bravado faltered. It had been a long time since I had done anything as reckless as a one-night stand, not to mention with my current er—ex-husband? I wasn't sure how to label him.

A fellow reader, Cami, gave me a knowing smile, and I felt my face blush. I guess we were more of a spectacle than I thought. I waved, then dipped into the restroom to splash water on my face. My light brown eyes were hooded with lust and my cheeks had a hint of dew to them.

I deserved this. I deserved one last night with him. I'll explain everything, and that will be it. We'll go our separate ways. I gave myself the pep talk as I walked over to the hotel next door. Coincidentally, the hotel I also had a room in. I barely noticed the opulent lobby or the crowd of people mingling around, or the music which played when I entered the elevator and hit the button for the penthouse. My awareness was focused on how quickly my heart was racing and the feeling of finally seeing my first love again.

The elevator door opened. I walked into a simple but elegant lobby, with only one door. Nerves fluttered in my belly. Hoping that this wasn't a set up and he actually was waiting for me, I knocked on the door. The door flung open, and Cole leaned against the door frame. We stood there in silence, our gazes locked, and his brown eyes filled with hunger. Cole glided his thumb against his bottom lip.

"I was going to give you one more minute before I came looking for you, kitten." His words were like whiskey—smooth, dark, and dangerous.

I took in a shuddered breath and smirked. "I guess I saved you the trouble."

Cole slowly shook his head as he took a step closer. "Oh kitten, I'm always in trouble when it comes to you."

FIVE

Cole

I THOUGHT I WAS DREAMING. That all my reminiscing about her was just that, a memory.

But when I saw her across the room in that tight black dress, with her silky, black hair in waves down her back, and her curvaceous body on display for anyone to see, my heart stopped. I believed my heart created an illusion. The moment I touched her, inhaled her scent of orange and vanilla, I knew it wasn't a dream. I didn't know how she managed to be in the same club I was in, but I didn't care. My wife was back in my arms. And I was going to punish her for leaving me.

Now that I have her, I was not letting her go. Parts of me warred - wanting her to hurt just like I did. Just like she did to me those years ago.

"You're so fucking beautiful, kitten." My stare slowly gazed up and down her body, taking in the minute changes of her breath. How her thighs seem to clench. How silky soft her brown skin was. Her light brown eyes darkened. I reached out and pulled her into me and slammed the door behind her. I walked us backward into the suite. Her curves molded perfectly to my body, just like it had over ten years ago. A bite of anger flashed through me, at the lost time. At what we missed out on. But I pushed it aside. Everything could be dealt with later. For now, my need to be with her outweighed everything else.

I wrapped one arm around her soft waist and gripped her jaw with my other hand. I bent down and barely touched her lips with mine.

"I have so many questions, Wife," I growled against her lips. I sank my teeth into her full bottom one. Her cry of pain had my already rock-solid cock thicken even more. I kept her gaze as I licked up the droplet of blood.

"Cole," she breathed. The sound of my name on her tongue made my cock weep with pre-cum.

I tightened my hold and moved my hand back to her throat. "I'm glad you remembered my name, Wife. Because you're going to be screaming it all night." I let her throat go, and she gave me the slightest frown, as if disappointed.

I smirked, my hands moved and gripped the hem of the dress that had been torturing me all night. She lifted her arms as I pulled the dress over her body. My mouth dropped as I stared at her in awe. Clad only in a black thong and heels, her sensuous tawny skin was in desperate need of my bite marks.

"Fuck, kitten. If you're not real, I don't want to wake up," I stepped into her space, cupped her face with my hands and crashed my lips to hers. I wanted to go gently. I wanted to warm her back to me. But the minute I saw her; primal instinct took over. My tongue demanded entry, sweeping in, and tasting the hint of tequila. My hands dropped to her waist, and I picked her up, wrapping her thick thighs around my waist. Our tongues clashed, messy and hedonistic. She arched her chest into mine, rolling her hips for only the friction I could give her.

"Cole," she pleaded, as my lips nibbled and sucked down her neck.

"Yes, my wife." I didn't recognize my own voice. I was desperate for her. I needed her cunt wrapped tightly around my cock. I needed to be so deep inside her so she'd never forget how I feel again. I walked over into my room and laid her down on my bed. I wanted to punish her. I wanted her to feel how I did ten years ago, when she left the sanctuary of the church we were holed up in during the hurricane, denying how she felt. I wanted to fuck her with nothing but rage and hate.

But I couldn't.

I needed to taste her. To feel her. To savor her. To remind her that even though we were twenty and nineteen years old, what we felt back then was real. That she was mine. She was the only one who ever truly held a hold on my heart.

My lips traced down her body, lathing her right nipple while squeezing her left breast. My teeth nibbled the underside of her breast, and I bit down gently, listening to her cues as she cried out in pleasure. My hand left her breast while my mouth continued to mark her, trailing down her soft waist to her black lace thong. My fingers roamed the soaked lace, outlining her lips.

"I missed you, kitten. You've been such a pain in my ass, making me wait for you. But fuck," I groaned. "A day didn't go by when I didn't miss the feel of you in my arms." I murmured softly. I laid everything out on the line. I normally held back, but with her, I couldn't let my emotions out fast enough.

"I missed you too, Cole," she moaned, her breaths coming faster the more I circled her wetness.

"I don't believe you." I ripped the drenched material off her and threw it over my shoulder. I ran my tongue up her inner thigh, gripping both thick limbs tightly as her breath hitched. Her scent of orange and musk sent my blood into a frenzy, and it took everything I had in me to not totally ravage her like a hungry man at a feast. My mouth watered, as I gazed at her glistening, silky, bare, brown pussy. I wasn't going to waste this opportunity, but she wasn't completely off the hook. She needed to be punished.

I smacked her pussy, surprising her as a yelp escaped.

"Cole!" she hissed.

I watched as her body shivered, and her pussy became wetter. Fuck. She liked it. "That's my fucking girl. I think my kitten likes being spanked," I purred. I smacked her again, my palm barely flinching at her engorged clit. A mixture of a groan and shriek came from her.

"Cole, please," she moaned. Damn if my dick didn't get harder at my name coming from her lips. My tongue traced her inner lips, tasting, nibbling, sucking. Her hands gripped at my head, pulling my strands as I continued my feast.

"You taste so fucking good, kitten," I moaned. I looked up and caught her gaze. She watched as I licked her slit, my tongue fucking her as I thrusted it inside her. Her tight cunt tightened around my tongue. I moved my hands under her ass and brought my meal up to my face, devouring her.

"Fuck!" she screamed, her glorious thighs tightened around my head. If I died of suffocation, I would have died a happy man. She came, her juices flowing into my mouth like a fucking geyser. And I made sure not to leave a drop.

I lifted my head and smiled at the beautiful sight before me. Sweat glistened along her brow. Her chest heaved and her eyes were half closed in ecstasy.

"I don't remember that," she mused with a smile.

"Baby girl, it's been a couple of years. I'm sure I learned a few new tricks," I smirked. I shucked off my dress pants, my dick springing out and smacking against my abs. I grabbed the base of my cock and pulled tightly, groaning at the sight before me. I stroked up the length of my cock, playing with the three barbells in my Jacob's ladder.

"You're pierced," she gasped, propping herself up on her elbows. Her brown eyes stared at my cock in wonderment. I just grinned, as it twitched in my hand.

"Yeah, baby. I am."

"I've never..."

"You've never, what? Been with a man who's been pierced?" I smirked.

She rolled her eyes at my smirk. That's right, baby. Give me one more reason to spank your delectable ass.

"No, I've never been with someone who is pierced."

"You're going to love it. I promise," I growled. Something pleased me inside, to know I was the first for her. I may not have been the only, but I was the only for right now. And if I had anything to say about it, I'd be her last.

I crawled on to the bed and up her luscious body. My hand curved around her thigh and wrapped it around my waist.

"There's no going back after this, kitten. About fucking time you realized you're mine." I lined myself up against her heat and slammed into her. Her scream only fueled my frenzy as my thrusts quickened. Her slick tightness gripped my cock like a fucking vice. It was everything I could do to hold back my orgasm. My fingers circled her clit as I adjusted my angle, hitting her in the spot that made her cunt quiver.

Her arms wrapped around my neck and drew me close. Her nails scratched down my back and I arched into the pain.

"God fucking damnit, kitten. You feel so fucking good." I drew back and watched as her beautiful breasts bounced with each thrust of my cock. "You're mine. Always have been, always will be."

"Cole." A low whine escaped her throat. She felt like heaven. Twenty-year old me couldn't even comprehend how fucking glorious this would be ten years later.

"I know baby, I know," I panted. I pulled out and smirked at her disappointed cry. "Oh baby. The sounds you make get me so fucking hard. Don't worry. I got you."

I flipped her onto her stomach, and gripped her hips, sliding back into her wet heat with a snarl. "God damn, you're so tight." I smacked her ass, my dick growing harder as her inner walls quivered. Her silky black hair was long enough to wrap around my fist. I gave into my urge, and pulled her hair back, having her arch into me as my other hand gripped her hip tightly. My thrusts quickened, encouraged by her whines and moans.

"Does that feel good, baby? Because I got to tell you, your cunt is sure as fuck hugging my cock." I grunted out.

"Cole. You feel so damn good," Evie rasped. Her muscles fluttered and clenched. Pressure built at the base of my spine and my balls tightened. Fuck. I needed her to come again before I made a fucking fool of myself.

I sat back on my heels, and pulled her back onto my lap, surging into her. My hand left her hair and reached around, finding her soft wet clit. Using her own slickness, I circled her clit with my thumb. Her low keen came to a high pitch, and she soaked my cock with a wail as she came.

"That's it, baby. That's it," I groaned. I couldn't hold back any longer. My vision blackened and I came with a roar. Her cries of ecstasy echoed throughout the room. My arms wrapped around her waist as her body went limp. My head bent forward and touched her dewy back. Our chests heaved; our breaths panted in unison. We were a mess of cum and sweat, but fuck it, I didn't want to move.

I gently pushed her forward and rolled her on to her back. I kissed her full lips slowly. I pulled back, and took her in. Her hair was plastered on her forehead as her chest heaved, her eyes heavy in exhaustion. She looked fucking beautiful. She looked like mine.

Begrudgingly, I pulled myself off the bed and made my way into my ensuite, where I cleaned myself up and wet a wash-cloth with warm water. I could tell sleep was mere moments away for Evie once I returned. My gaze lingered at the apex of her thighs. My cum glistened on her inner thighs and my cock twitched in anticipation. This wasn't going to be the last time. I gently cleaned her up, then climbed into the bed, pulling the sheets over us.

She wrapped herself around me, unknowingly, with her head tucked into the crook of my neck and her leg tucked in between mine. My arm held her close and for a moment, I let myself just be there. In the present. No brooding about the past or worrying about what shit storm we'll be walking into next week.

Just here, with her. Where I've wanted to be for god knows how long. There were other women, but none held my heart and soul the way she did. And now that I had her back, I was never letting her go again.

She was mine. Whether she wanted to be or not.

SIX

Evie

WHEN YOU CAN'T BLAME the alcohol, can you blame the hormones?

That was my first thought when I opened my eyes to the still dark room. My body was deliciously sore. For the briefest of moments, I felt content. Sated. Loved. But guilt and regret quickly replaced those feelings and pushed away any other feeling I had. Cole's arms were around my waist, and he held me close, as if he was preventing me from running away. But I knew I couldn't stay. Not with everything going on back at home. I couldn't bring him into the mess I was in. It wouldn't be fair to him or to his family I knew he was close to. But Syndicate isn't a group to fuck around with, and if anyone is going down with the ship, it's going to be me. I'm not bringing anyone else with me.

I loosened his grip and slid off the bed, holding my breath. I hated leaving him like this. I hated leaving him at all and for a split moment, I wanted to tell him everything. Why I left him in Mexico. Why I never reached out to him and ghosted him for years. Why I had to leave now. But I couldn't do it. Knowing Cole, he would fight for me and damn if I didn't want him to risk his life. I wanted someone to fight for me. But this was way too dangerous. The situation I was in was extremely deadly, and there's nothing anyone else could do.

Once the Syndicate is decimated, I will come back to you. I vowed. I quietly pulled on the dress, stuffed my panties in the clutch and slowly tip-toed out of the room with my heels in hand. I closed the door behind me with a soft click. I was too caught up in Cole last night to take a look around the opulence of the room. There was a large dining table with a large kitchenette with a full size fridge. A living room with a U-shaped couch filled the space between Cole's bedroom and another what I would assume to be bedroom. I took a moment to sit and slide on my shoes. I didn't worry about making myself presentable. I was only going down ten floors, so my walk-of-shame wouldn't be as obvious.

"I guess sneaking away from him is going to be your habit?" A familiar voice murmured. I gave a startled gasp and looked toward the window. With a view of the Nashville skyline, I didn't notice a man standing there. A very familiar man, wearing nothing but a pair of gym shorts and a pair of thick black glasses.

"Fuck. Zeke, what the hell are you doing here?" I whisper shouted, throwing a glance at Cole's door.

"Making sure my boy doesn't leave with a broken heart. Did you really think I wouldn't have done my due diligence before I first approached you?"

Fuck.

I didn't tell Maks, but I had been feeding Zeke information for years. Zeke found me when I was trying to discreetly reach out to a trafficking survivors' group. He saw something in me, the good I wanted to do. He didn't know me as the frivolous daughter of a finance crime-lord. He knew but saw past it. Zeke gave me a lot. He gave me the encrypted burner phone so I could make the necessary calls and equipment to keep myself and my tech secure. But even more so, he gave me the courage to do what I needed to do.

A thought crossed my mind. "Shit—does that mean Cole is a part of your team?" My panic rose. I never wanted him to be part of this shit show. He didn't deserve to be dragged into my mess.

Zeke could tell my anxiety was heightened. "He is a part of my team, but I have kept your identity a secret." His large frame crossed the expansive distance and grasped my biceps in a firm, but tender way. "You're good, Raven. You're okay."

"He can't know." My breath quickened as my chest heaved.

"Raven," Zeke gently admonished.

"We're pretty much besties now, Zeke. You can use my name," I snapped quietly. I bared a glance over my shoulder at Cole's closed door. "I need to go."

"Rav—I mean, Evie. Listen." Zeke started.

"No. You listen. He's the one of the few great things in my convoluted life, and I'm not having him wrapped up in this shit show. Do not fucking tell him," I gritted out. I yanked myself out of his arms and hurried over to the elevator.

"I think you'd find Cole would be beneficial in your corner. He's your husband, after all." Zeke replied with a smirk.

I gave him a glare. "You know we're not really married."

"Does he know that?" I arched my eyebrow in disbelief. There's no way in hell Cole would remain celibate for the past ten years. Cole rolled his eyes and held up his hands in mock surrender.

"Fine. You're right. I'll keep it quiet. And we're still a go for Tuesday. I'll have someone at the bar," he said. I nodded and pressed the button rapidly. Thankfully, I didn't have to wait long before it came, and I was able to head down three floors to my room.

I checked my phone. It was only four in the morning, and my flight wasn't until noon the next day. Fuck it. I logged into the airline app and changed my flight to one leaving at eight-thirty in the morning. There was no reason for me to stick around now and I didn't want to chance running into Zeke or Cole again. I quickly showered and changed into a pair of light gray joggers, and a crop top hoodie, then threw my clothes and toiletries into my suitcase. I quickly gathered all the books and merchandise I purchased from the book event into my carry-on. I ordered an Uber, then checked the room for any random bits. I always tended to leave a charger or something behind, but for some reason, I wanted to make sure I didn't leave a trace of me behind. My moment of peace was gone, and it was time to go back to the madness that was my life.

I made my way down to the lobby, then to the airport without any issues. By the time I pulled up to my small, old, Craftsman style home five hours later, I was beyond exhausted. I just wanted to go in and sleep for twenty-four hours. Between the book event and the meeting up with Cole, my head was pounding and my hangover was getting the better of me. Thankfully, Angela and Chris from across the street kept the fat king entertained, fed, and happy. They sent me pictures of his royal highness, and I was grateful he had the loving atten-tion of the family and kids. After giving Mario his mandatory snuggles, and dinner, I ordered food from the restaurant up the street and took another shower to get off all the travel gunk.

Of course, once the buffalo chicken sub from Mac & Bobs arrived, the little shit thought he had ownership of my food too.

I ate while ignoring his plaintive pleas and went through the inventory order that was legitimately supposed to come this week. The regular shipment of beer, food, and hard liquor we needed in order to feed our customers. The order coincided with the order of whomever was in the truck Sebastian had coming. I made sure everything was up to date, but that was all I could do. Clients confirmed their upcoming orders and the payments were received. My stomach felt tight, due to a mix of food and disgust. I put away the left of my meal, much to Mario's dismay, and checked my supplies. When the first truckful of women and children came through, I was caught off guard. They needed so many basic supplies, items infants needed to survive. It made me sick not being able to help them fully. I finally convinced Sebastian healthy women and babies would garner a higher price, and he finally allowed me to purchase the very bare minimum. At least for the children. The women, it seemed the more they were beaten and drugged up, the better.

I wasn't a hundred percent sure of what sort of product we were to receive, but I could only assume infants were involved. My gut twisted and I wanted to throw up. I wasn't sure how much more of this I could stomach. I had to focus on putting my emotions aside and put on the mask of The Broker. I paid for overnight delivery and closed my laptop. My emotional spoons were too full. There wasn't much more I could do except to mentally prepare myself for the shit storm that was about to take place. I was grateful for Zeke's team, but the deep, cynical part of me didn't think anything would come to fruition.

It was only a matter of time before the Syndicate was taken down. But the question remained—at what cost?

SEVEN

Cole

Of all the missions I have done, sitting in a bar in some podunk town, listening to country music while drinking a weak-ass IPA, wasn't the worst. The rescue operation in the jungles of Brazil, while fighting off mosquitos and poisonous snakes, and Amazonian tribes who hated outsiders, probably was the worst. There were other ways I would rather spend my time. I would prefer to be in bed with my wife. But that was unrealistic. Three weeks ago, I was curled up with her in Nashville. Only to wake up and have her gone.

Again.

Fuck it. Part of me was pissed, and I couldn't tell if I was more pissed off at her or if I was angrier with myself. That's her MO. She's a fucking runner. A damned coward to not face me. But I had to smile. I so loved a good chase. My kitten had another thing coming, if she thought I was going to give up that easily. I was nothing but persistent. I made the mistake of not chasing her ten years ago. I wasn't going to make the same mistake again.

So instead of hunting down my wife and putting her over my knee, I was following a lead on a trafficking ring that led to outside of Roanoke, Virginia. Someone named the Broker was arranging the deliveries and pickups of women. Zeke's informant provided the intel, then went black. Zeke mandated someone come out and since I was the only one free, I was voluntold.

I checked the clock on the wall and inwardly groaned. It was seven minutes behind my normal schedule, and there was only so long I could nurse this nasty beer without calling attention to myself. No man worth his balls would sip on his drink like it was a baby bottle. And I didn't need the extra attention. It didn't help I was a stranger in a small town, at six-three and two thirty, covered in tattoos. I was already a walking red flag.

I sat at the bar in my uniform of dirty jeans, mud-covered boots, and a long-sleeved tee. My worn ball hat covered my eyes and I didn't speak to anyone except to order a beer and a plate of fries. I kept to myself. As far as anyone could tell, I was a laborer working on the big road construction project in the next town over. I had been coming to random bars in this town around eight-thirty at night every night for the past week, slowly letting the locals get used to me. I wanted to blur into the background and allow my presence to become part of the daily noise.

I did the same thing every day to build up the pattern and complacency. I left my rented apartment at five in the morning and drove through town to the local bakery where I would pick up a breakfast sandwich, a donut, and a coffee. Although, with the way my jeans were fitting, I think I needed to cut back on the donuts.

From there, I would ostensibly go to the work site. The job

was big enough to where I could easily disappear within the workforce. But really, I swapped out my car at a midpoint location and headed into the woods. This area was one of the main arteries of a human trafficking route and according to Zeke's sources, this was the spot where the women and children went missing. Someone in this town knew what was going on and based on the clientele, I would bet a billion donuts that finding someone to talk to would be harder than finding a hooker who just wanted to cuddle for free.

I glanced at my watch and sighed. I stood up and threw down a twenty and caught the eye of the old bartender. I lifted my chin, then headed for the door. I pushed on the old wooden door just as someone pulled it open, and a small hard body slammed into me with an oof. I immediately braced my hands on her shoulders before she could bounce back and fall.

"Oh fuck, sorry about that," she muttered. My gaze quickly snapped to hers as she tilted her head up. Her brown eyes were the color of honey, and I could easily see how someone could get lost in them. Because I did twice. And the last time was three weeks ago.

Her eyes widened with recognition and a small gasp escaped her beautiful, plump lips. It took everything in my power not to respond. My jaw tightened. I pulled myself out of the trance and gave her a short nod, then stepped around her to leave the bar, letting the door close behind me. I climbed into my basic, black pickup truck, and started her up. The battle within myself was difficult. The urge to keep her curvy, petite, frame against mine warred against the raging need for answers. Her being here changed everything. I shook my head and pulled out of the crowded parking lot, headed toward the outskirts of town.

In the privacy of my car, I took some deep breaths. I

couldn't overreact. I had to think this through. Why, of all the towns in the fucking country, was she here?

I grabbed a greasy dinner from the closest burger joint and made it back to the apartment. Home away from home. It's been weeks since I have seen my actual home. Home was a small house in the Baltimore suburbs, not an old, run-down motel that probably saw its share of drama and despots. It was outdated with its dark floral bedspread, stiff sheets, and questionable minifridge. But it was clean, cheap, and most importantly, out of the way. But it didn't have my best buddy, who was living his best life with Charlie and Sketch.

I debated about showering before I ate, but my stomach argued against it. I flipped on the encrypted laptop and sat down at the small round table. I took a bite of my burger while the machine booted up.

I flipped open my encrypted phone and dialed the one number I had for Zeke.

"Mind telling why I had a run-in with my wife?" I growled into the phone as I shoved another fry in my mouth. I cursed myself for not picking up a bottle of whiskey or a six pack of beer, because the fries weren't helping my stress level.

"Well hello to you too, Cole. How's the recon going?" Zeke's deep voice came through and I rolled my eyes.

"Look, fucker. Tell me why I am doing recon on this op and I run into Evie. *My Evie.* Is she a part of this?" I snapped.

Zeke sighed, as if he dreaded this conversation. "Look man. I didn't know she was your wife when I first approached her."

Rage hit my veins and it took everything in me to not throw the phone against the thin wall. "You fucking approached my wife to be your informant?"

"She was trying to reach out to Rainbow Trail when I picked up her digital dust. After she made contact with Brittny, I approached her. She has the access, and she wanted to help."

Zeke replied, calmly. As if he was trying to ward off the verbal attack he knew was about to come.

"And you let her. You let her continue this fucking charade? She could be killed!"

"I know that. She knows that. She's more damn stubborn than you are, so I'm sure that's what brought you together," Zeke replied calmly.

"Jeez, man. This...this isn't right. What's her story, Zeke? What's she doing here?" The desperation in my voice was slight, but I'm sure Zeke could hear it.

"Cliffs Notes version? She has the most access we could have ever asked for. She married Makism Alexyandez, the nephew of Dmitri Alexyandez, the pakhan of the Alexyandez Bratva and her daddy's best friend. And dude, you truly didn't do your due diligence. Her folks aren't clean, either. They've both built empires in the financial and commercial real estate worlds. Her father is a Papa Smurf."

Fuck. Not referring to the '80s cartoon, smurfing was a term that referred to the practice of avoiding regulatory scrutiny by dividing large sums of money into multiple smaller transactions and accounts. In other words, an intricate practice of money laundering.

"They launder money, using commercial properties to do so," I surmised.

"Among other shady business dealings, but yep." He popped that "p" loudly, and I gritted my teeth.

"For who?"

"Let's put it a better way. Who didn't he help? Her folks are Andres and Isla Banks. They don't work for just one group or organization. They work with them all. They have their hands in so many pots and move money in such a convoluted and legit way, no one government can touch it. The Banks know way too much and where the bodies are buried. That's what keeps them around."

Fuck. "I can't believe Evie is the daughter of the Bankers." Their reputation was prominent. Isla and Andres Banks, otherwise known as the Bankers, were slippery to touch. Members of all the levels of government were in their back pocket, not to mention CEOs and corporate executives. No evidence sticks and it's normally gone before a case ever comes to light. It's a known secret Andres Banks was also known as Papa Smurf on the dark web.

"Yeah, about that. How the hell did you not know your own wife's last name? I thought I taught you better," Zeke scoffed. I heard the rustling of papers behind him.

"Fuck you, dick. It's not like I got to spend a whole time getting to know her. We had almost two weeks together, and most of that was..." Wonderful. Sensual. The best fucking weeks of my life. When I traveled down to Sayulita after my first deployment, I was only looking for rest and relaxation. I planned on spending my days surfing and my nights finally catching up on my sleep. I never thought I would find the woman that would steal my heart.

"Yeah, the sun, surf, and sex vacay," Zeke replied dryly.

"Obviously the op has changed," I stated. There was no doubt it was a command versus a suggestion.

"Um, no. The fuck it has. Mission remains the same. Take control of the Broker, pull the thread, and untangle the Syndicate," Zeke ordered.

"You're fucking joking. You honestly think I'm going to sit back and watch as the Syndicate brings her down in this whole bullshit scenario. You're out of your damn mind." Fury rang in my voice and it took me several breaths to calm down. The idea of Evie, the beautiful and pure hearted Evie, sitting with the most vile and disgusting humans ever, enraged a beast I hadn't felt in a very long time.

"You're joking if you think your relationship with Evie has any bearing on this mission. You have your orders, Cole. Don't deviate," snapped Zeke.

"This isn't your fucking decision, Zeke!"

"You're right. It's not. I cleared it with Noah. Noah says it's a go, so it's a fucking go."

Fuck. While we make operational decisions as a team, Noah had the highest rank out of all of us and had the final approval. He was the voice of reason that Sketch and I needed. Most of the time. Right now, I definitely didn't agree.

"I'm not letting my wife get involved in this!" I shouted and banged my fist on the coffee table.

"Do you honestly think Evie would take orders from anyone? She's been involved since day one. The shit she knew, the information she's passed along, that's why she's doing this. Evie knows the risks she's taking and despite me trying to bring her in, she has refused!" Zeke shot back. Angry breaths came through the phone, and I knew I had pushed him over the edge. "Fuck man, ever since I met her, I've felt something ..." I growled, not liking the way this was going. "For God's sake. Stop. Yes, she's gorgeous and any man worth his nuts would love to be between those beautiful thighs. But once I dug deeper, I realized who she was. More like—who she was to you. But regardless, she's in. She knows what she's doing."

"Why the fuck didn't you tell me? Once you figured out who she was, why didn't you tell me?" I muttered, defeated. To know she's been involved with this bullshit, to not be able to protect her, drove my primal side crazy.

"I admit, it took a while to figure out you were together ten years ago. But I couldn't tell you, even once I knew. Because you only spoke about your Evie when you were totally drunk and broody. And when I saw her in Nashville —"

"You saw her in Nashville? When?"

"I first met her up in the garden to deliver info. And then I caught her sneaking out after your...escapade."

"But you never said anything. I've been racking my brain to figure out where the hell she was but you let her fucking leave?"

"What did you say to me when you finally woke up and came out into the suite? Not a damn thing. You didn't ask if I saw her. You didn't ask where she was. You barely looked at the fucking door until it was time to leave. And honestly? She told me not to tell you. Because of this. Because she knew you would flip your shit and go bat shit crazy. But Cole, man, she grew up in this life. She's the daughter of a fucking Smurf, bro. She may have grown up blind to what's going on, but her eyes are wide open now. Her reports and marks have saved countless women and children," Zeke replied, his tone softening.

My screaming need to protect her raged against the truth in his words. The amount of women we've saved or funneled through The Rainbow Trial, a human trafficking safety net, was unbelievable. People in the county had no clue this country was a hotbed for human smugglers, for all age ranges. Our teams stick to the background and help transport the survivors to the transit points, but after that—we never hear how they thrive or if they fall back into the system.

"I don't like it." I muttered, rubbing a weary hand over my five-day-old scruff.

"I know. I don't either. But you have to fucking deal with it. Now give me the update."

"The update is there's no update. It's quiet as a mouse. There hasn't been any movement in town, I haven't found any trails or sites that could be holding areas." All I've found is my wife.

"We know that the shipment Evie had expected a few weeks ago never came through. And with the exception of one text, she's been radio silent."

"Is this where Evie's located? Is this where she's working out of?" I was desperate to find out any information about her. The more I had, the more I could protect her.

"Yes. Smokey's Bar and Grill is under her name, but the entire building belongs to belongs to Maks's uncle. The shop next to it? That's BCG, the custom rims and parts place Shane said belonged to the Cruz Cartel. This is the first transit point for their inventory. Having you out there, as back up, is going to be crucial next time there's a shipment."

"Why now? We've been intercepting these shipments without issue for months." I frowned. We let them go through the transition stops and capture the shipments once they're a couple of states away.

Zeke paused. "Yeah, but like I said the other day, something is off. The chatter about any shipments is now done offline so I haven't been able to determine what's going on. Evie hasn't been able to get a read out on any sort of schedule or process. She's completely blind to everything now. We need another set of eyes on the situation. And with Noah and Kate finally back from their honeymoon, and Sketch coming back from upstate New York, we're able to take a closer look."

"Wouldn't someone like Benji, whose specialty was technical surveillance, be better suited for this?" Another pregnant pause. "You sonofabitch. You knew if I found Evie here, I wouldn't leave."

"Was I wrong?" The smugness in his voice made me want to hit something. As much as I loved him, the bastard needed to be knocked into the next week.

"No, you're not fucking wrong, you damn dickhead. Now what's the timeline? How long am I here for?"

"Until something happens. We have Torin, Benji, and Trey taking points along the major routes, and the JV team is filling in where needed," Zeke's smug tone fills the air. "I hope you brought extra drawers."

"You're going to pay for this," I grumbled.

"Think about it this way. You're now able to finally talk to your wife."

"You know we're not legally married."

"Funny. That's what she said in Nashville. It's whatever, but if I need to draw you up some back-dated papers declaring you were, I can."

"Whatever, dick. I'll figure it out."

"Keep your eyes open. I know it's going to suck having you out there, but I have a feeling something big is coming.

"Got it." I hung up with Zeke and rubbed my eyes. After being a ghost for ten years, Evie was now only twenty minutes away. My heart warred with my brain once more. As angry and pissed off I was about her leaving me twice, my heart craved her.

Looks like fate has finally turned in my direction. I closed up my system and put it all into a bag, locking it up. Even if someone were to try and break in, it's completely secure and they wouldn't be able to get in without my biometric data. I jumped into the shower and washed off the grime, only to get out and pull on another pair of jeans and a hooded sweatshirt. I grabbed my keys and my ball cap and rocked out the door.

Now that I knew where she was, there was no way in hell I was going to let her go. Not without a fight.

EIGHT

Evie

OF COURSE. The first day I'm back from Mexico visiting my sick abuela, and I was called into the bar because Arnie, the other bartender, needed to leave early. It was a shit day anyway, due to my period starting and my hot water heater dying. All I wanted to do was relax with a pizza and some Bridgerton, but duty called. I was just going in to close the drawers, because Lord knew Dmitri would have slipped a few dollars into his pockets. I didn't want to go into work, but hell, all I needed was the Syndicate to pitch a fit because I wasn't pulling my weight.

And to be fair, my mind was still on that night back in Nashville. It had been three weeks since I saw Cole, and I couldn't stop thinking about him. I irritated at the world. Angry at myself for allowing the whole night to happen, but at the same time, for not talking with him. For continuing with this whole saga and how my life had turned out.

Of course, fate had other plans. Running into Cole at my bar was never on my bingo card but here we were. I internally shook off the shock of seeing him and shuffled behind the wooden counter. The bar was busier than I expected, but running the drinks and closing out tabs didn't do much for taking my mind off our run-in. My thoughts wandered to our night in Nashville. Did he know I was here this entire time? I waffled between wanting him to come back and hoping he stayed away.

Focus Evie. This wasn't the time to be thinking about our relationship—or whatever the hell it was called. There were more important things to worry about. The vibe in the bar has changed in the last couple of weeks, and it made me weary. While I didn't want to get him involved, I even knew when to ask for help.

The shipments Sebastian had been boasting about have been sporadic, at best. The shipments show up randomly, without any order or schedule. And whatever the product is, whether it be guns, drugs, or humans, it's moved quickly, barely sticking around for more than an hour. The clients had been arranged without my help, wire payments had been sent. There has been no preparation, or quality control checks. Sebastian hasn't involved me. Normally I would be happy with the lack of trafficking, but with all the bluster and pomp about my assistance and expertise, Sebastian had been suspiciously close mouthed.

I've kept up my ruse, ignoring everything and pretending to pay no mind to the shipments. Sebastian was not shy in demanding my assistance, and it would have been out of character for me to suddenly offer my help. I've been keeping Zeke and his crew up to date with random texts and cryptic social media posts about books. Zeke also sent out some listening devices, by care of my P.O. Box in the next town over. I had managed to place a couple, but I had one remaining. Sebastian was a paranoid genius, so I was sure they would be picked up on any of the technical sweeps they do, which was my greatest fear.

My assumption was Cole was here to get a better read out on the situation. But his lack of background, plus the inability to blend in with the rest of the town showed he wouldn't be able to get anything more than I would be able to provide. If I, the one on the ground, couldn't determine when and where our next shipment would be, then how the hell would Cole find out?

The whole situation frustrated the hell out of me. It was like a clock was ticking down and I was on edge waiting for something to happen. For something major to happen. This was the worst kind of edging, I thought grimly, as I wiped down the bar.

At times like these, I wished I had someone to confide in. Macie lived three hours from me, and normally I was grateful she was away from this chaos. But right now, I really needed to talk to my best friend. But what could I have told her? That the man I gave my soul to when I was eighteen is now back in my life? And oh by the way, he's investigating a human trafficking ring that I'm an accomplice to? Any variation of the truth would either cause more questions or put her in danger. That was something I was not willing to do.

"You hungry? I'm about to close the grill," Rocco rumbled, as he brought out a plate of popcorn chicken and his freshly made potato chips for the bouncers.

"Yeah. I could eat. Could I get a West Coast Club?" My mouth watered at the thought of Rocco's club sandwiches. The man smokes all his own meats, so the bacon and turkey were always fresh. He's the only reason why I haven't starved since moving out here.

"Fries?"

"Sweet potato?" I asked hopefully. I filled a glass with his favorite hard cider and handed it over to him. "My favorite for yours?"

Rocco rolled his eyes and stalked away with his drink in his hand. I glanced at the antique clock behind the bar. It was already ten at night. There were only a couple of stragglers left, and they were the locals who pretty much left when we did.

"Hey, Ivan. Let's start clearing out. Rocco's about done in the kitchen, so once he's ready, we can roll," I called out. I pulled out the drawer for the second register and started counting it out. There wasn't much left to do tonight, so Ivan and Jimmy picked up the bar-back duties. Everything was refilled for the next day and the dishes were put away. I put the money into the safe and shoved the ledger and laptop from the office into my bookbag. I'd rather pay the bills and do inventory in my comfy pajamas, where I could freak out in the privacy of my own home. As I made my way back down the dark hallway to the bar, Rocco popped out of the kitchen with a plastic bag stuffed to the brim.

"That's a lot for a turkey club," I joked. I took the bag and tested the weight. It was pretty heavy.

"It's a turkey club and fries, plus some leftover meatballs and noodles. You know your sorry self won't cook. And some of the damn cheesecake you won't shut up about. We just got a shipment in." Rocco was bitter I was addicted to a dessert that wasn't his. I met Natacha at a book event, and we hit it off right away. And while she lived in upstate New York, she was one of my best friends. Plus, her cheesecakes in a jar were the best thing ever. We struck a deal, and now I get to sell her Lick Your

Lips Cheesecakes at the bar. Of course, I always made sure I got my sample first.

"You know you can stop lying. I saw you sneaking a jar of her bourbon waffle cheesecake last week. You looked so blissed out; I didn't want to interrupt." The blush fainted across his olive skin tone as he grumbled ambled toward the back.

"Thank you, Rocco!" I called behind him. He waved me away as he walked back through the swinging kitchen doors.

"Ready to go, boss?" Ivan looked up from his phone.

"Yeah. Is the other shop still open?" I asked, as I locked the door.

"Yeah. We have a full house tonight," he murmured. A full house meant a Syndicate meeting. With Sebastian as one of the leaders of the Cruz Cartel, he was also the de facto leader of the Syndicate. He had his fingers in all of the pots. Which meant there were always a bunch of unsavory folks in the shop next door. Folks I didn't want any part of.

"Still on those dating apps, I see," I mused, as I hurried out the door, nodding to the phone in his hand.

Ivan smirked, his blue eyes not really moving from the app, as he held the door for me. "Well, just trying to find someone new."

I chuckled as I headed to my SUV. "You mean to tell me there could actually be someone you haven't dicked in the entire area of Salem?"

Ivan had the decency to look away sheepishly. "I mean, it's a new school year, right? I'm sure there are some transfer students..." I held up my hand and stopped him right there.

"What you do on your own time is your business. Just make sure they're legal and it's consensual." I patted him on the cheek lightly. "This isn't the life you should be living. I know you're better than that. Treat the girls like you'd want your wife to be treated."

Ivan blushed. "Ya, Ma. I gotchu." Out of all the men in the outfit I worked with, Ivan was the one I looked after like a brother. He was younger than me by eight years, so he was still a baby in some way. He was a good kid. If he could get away from Sebastian and Dmitri, his future would be a lot brighter.

"Behave yourself." I gave him a smile and climbed into the SUV.

"Behave myself? Never." He grinned. I smiled back at him and pressed the button to start the SUV. Nothing happened but a clicking sound.

"Hey Ivan? Something..."

"Fuck!" I was suddenly pulled from the car and into Ivan's arms, and a split second later, we were both flung across the yard as the SUV exploded. I landed with a thud on my stomach, my head hitting the ground hard. Gravel and debris fell on my body, shards of glass. My head pulsed. My ears rang and I couldn't focus. My vision blurred.

"Ivan?" I whispered. Even that low tone pained my ears. The heat across my back was almost blistering and I struggled to get up. A sharp pain ricocheted through my body, and I collapsed once more on the ground. I heard shouts but I couldn't tell what they were saying. My mouth was too dry, like it was full of dirt, to yell for help. Suddenly, I was lifted and moved. Shouts gave way to gunfire, as the sound of peppering bullets filled the night air.

I moaned as I was jostled again. Sleep was pulling me under, and I closed my eyes.

"Nah, kitten. You're going to want to keep those pretty honey eyes open for me." A familiar voice cracked through the pounding in my head. I knew his voice. It was a voice I had been dreaming about for the last few weeks.

"Cole," I groaned. I tried to turn my head toward the

warmth of his body, but his hold tightened enough to where I couldn't move.

"Stay still, kitten. Stay fucking still. You could have a head injury," he muttered. His movements slowed and he laid me on the wet grass, a ways away from the chaos.

"Look at me. Open those pretty eyes." His breath crossed my face, the scent of mint a welcome relief from the scent of burning rubber and gasoline. I struggled to answer his demand, but eventually, my eyelashes flickered open. His face was covered in a full-face black ski mask, but I'd recognize those brown eyes anywhere.

"Cole," I breathed. His hand came up and cupped my cheek and for a moment, I let myself linger in his touch. But reality suddenly fell over me. "You need to get out of here," I attempted to sit up but his hand on my sternum gently held me down.

"Oh, don't worry. I'm leaving, and you're going with me. I need to make sure you don't have a concussion or something," He flashed a pen light in my eyes. "You need to be checked out."

"No, Cole. Seriously. Get out of here. They can't see you here." I moaned, swatting his hand away.

"You're coming with me."

"I can't. They'll kill both of us if I leave here with you. I have a job, let me fucking finish it," I snapped, my teeth clenched with the pain.

"Your job fucking sucks, kitten. And they won't touch you. I'm calling for backup."

I managed to roll over to my stomach and pushed myself up onto my knees. "If they find you here, they will kill you. They will kill me for being with you, and they'll kill your entire family. You know what they're capable of. I've been doing this for years. Let me finish this damn job." I growled. I couldn't look at his face, I couldn't look him in the eyes. My resolve would have crumbled if I did.

"I'm not fucking leaving you." The anguish in his voice finally made me look up.

"You have to," I whispered a sigh and a wince. I closed my eyes and willed him to see this my way. This was the only way we would both survive.

Shouts echoed from close by, and I watched Cole battle with himself. With a curse, he stood up. "I'll be watching you. You're not getting away from me again, Evie." He bent down and brushed his lips against mine. "I'll see you later."

With a final look, he ran off into the shadows of the trees.

"Evie! Boss! Are you okay?" Rocco came limping over. A bloody gash was across his forehead and his arm was at an odd angle.

"What the hell happened, Rocco?" I muttered, as I struggled to get up. Rocco yelled for the other crew, and three guys came running over. "Where's Ivan?"

Rocco frowned and shook his head gently. Fuck. Tears filled my eyes and coursed down my cheeks. He saved me at the cost of himself.

Rocco put his hand under my arm and helped me stand up. My body swayed as I gathered my bearings.

"What the hell happened?" I repeated. I closed my eyes to stop the dizziness. But my nausea didn't abate.

"An ambush. Two gunmen. They came out after your car exploded. We took them out though." I leaned on Rocco, and we held each other up, while looking around at all of the chaos unfolding. Sebastain's hulking figure was bellowing orders, and his minions were running around, extinguishing the flames from the car.

"Why my SUV?" I wondered out loud. No other vehicles

were targeted, and mine sure as hell wasn't as fancy as the other ones in the lot.

"Who knows. Here comes the boss man." Rocco grumbled. My eyes wandered over to see Sebastian making his way over to where we stood in the grass.

His eyes perused both of us, scrutinizing our injuries. Sebastian's face hardened and his sharp jawline was clenched. "Looks like you're alive. But those fuckers who tried to swing at me aren't." He surveyed the damage from our vantage point. "I don't know who the hell you pissed off, but your SUV is toast. The attention this is causing will be unfortunate and is going to take a lot of money to brush aside."

No how are you or how are you feeling? Just straight to the point on how a potential ambush inconvenienced him. Not that I expected anything different. Almost accusatory in his tone, I wanted to brush him off but my smart mouth didn't get the memo.

"Maybe it was the clientele you've been keeping?" I offered snidely. Shit. I immediately regretted the words as soon as they passed my lips.

"That clientele pays your salary and keeps your damn bar afloat. And might I remind you, my customers are your customers too, which makes this your problem as well," Sebastian seethed. The control he was holding on to was about to snap, and I had the presence of mind to keep my snarkiness in check.

I glanced around at the damage. "Speaking of your clientele, was anyone else injured?" I deflected. If I actually responded to his remarks, everything I had worked for would be over with. Because I would be dead due to sass.

Sebastian rolled his eyes. "A few soldiers were taken out, but their demise is their own fault. They should have been more observant."

The coldness of these words was part of his MO. He was a psychopath and his lack of respect for those who put themselves in the way of danger was par for the course.

I nodded slightly, the pain hurting my body and my head. I closed my eyes as my head throbbed.

"I'm just going to take Evie home," Rocco replied grimly. He put his arm around my waist and started to lead me toward his vehicle.

"No. Rocco, you head to the medic. Jimmy. Take Evelyn home. She's no use to us here," Sebastian sneered.

Jimmy hustled over, covered in dirt and soot. He wrapped his arm around my waist, holding my weight against him. We started to shuffle toward his truck.

"Oh Evelyn." His cold voice had me freeze. "You need to be careful. We don't need another incident like Maks."

My insides froze and I nodded numbly, as Jimmy led me toward his sedan.

"You need to get seen by a doctor," I mumbled. Jimmy leaned me against the car while he got the door open.

"Same to you, Ma," he replied. I sank into the front seat and let him close the door. My head leaned against the window during the entire drive back to my place. I wanted to close my eyes and forget about what happened. But I needed to keep my wits about me. Someone tried to kill me tonight. The question was who was the primary target? While it could have very well been some nemesis of the Syndicate, the whole situation seemed very lackluster for a raid when there were heads of multiple crime families gathered in one area.

My head pounded and I pushed any sort of critical thinking away. I needed sleep, water, and something for my head. I couldn't tell the difference in time, but we made the trek back to my home rather quickly. The house was dark, just as I left it. But it was a bit nerve racking.

Jimmy sensed my anxiety. "I'll check out the place before you go in." He put his hands out for the keys, and I placed them in his palm. I wasn't about to protest. My paranoia was already running my mind ragged. I watched as each light in my home turned on one by one, and soon after, he came out to my door.

"I didn't see any issues, aside from a very mean cat. He almost tore my arm off." I smirked at the thought of fifteen-pound Mario terrifying a grown-ass adult.

"Didn't realize you were afraid of a little pussy," I muttered as he helped me out of his truck.

"I will drop you dead ass on the ground." He glared at me. "I ain't afraid of pussy. But that cat has extra toes. And he stood up on his hind legs and growled at me when I walked into the kitchen. That's a damn alien in your house. Like the cartoon from Disney."

"You mean Lilo and Stitch?" I mused dryly.

"Yeah, That." He opened the door and helped me inside, and across the short distance over to my gray sectional sofa. I sat gingerly on the cushion and glanced at Jimmy, as he awkwardly rubbed the back of his neck.

"Uh... Erm. Do you need anything?"

I snorted. "You're good, bub. Go ahead and roll out. Thanks for bringing me home." Jimmy's dark eyebrow arched in disbelief, and I shooed him away with my hands.

"All right. Text me if you need anything," Jimmy said sheepishly, as he walked out the door. The silence that followed his departure was welcomed, but also unnerving. The ringing in my ears lessened, but the throbbing in my head and body continued. I stood up gingerly and shuffled into the kitchen. Mario's cries for his dinner went ignored as I went for the pain reliever in the cabinet. The generic brand of aceta-minophen would have to suffice.

"Kitten, you need to be sitting down."

"Fuck!" The bottle dropped onto the counter and the red and blue pills scattered. My heart felt like it was pounding out of my chest. I turned around and glared at the six-foot-something man standing in the doorway of my pantry.

"Are you for real right now? What are you doing here, Cole?" I groaned. I started to gather the fallen pills to put away, when he came over next to me. His sandalwood and whiskey scent enveloped me. I wanted to blame the concussion, but I knew what really made my knees weak.

"We have shit to discuss, and I told you I'm not letting you out of my sight." His brown eyes searched my body, looking for injuries. "What hurts?"

"Right now, my patience. I don't have any with you," I grumbled, as I wrestled with the cap to the water bottle. My body throbbed and I leaned into the counter for support.

"Shush. I got you." His warmth surrounded me as he pulled me into his chest, wrapping his arms around me like a comfortable blanket. My knees buckled, but he swooped me into his arms and held me close, bringing me back to the couch.

"I'm okay," I managed.

"Keep lying to someone else. I know better," Cole murmured. He laid me back down on the couch. "Stay here."

If it didn't kill my head, I would have rolled my eyes. "Bossy as hell," I muttered.

"I heard that," he called from the kitchen.

"I meant for you to." My energy was draining from my body. I wanted to take some pain meds, take a shower, and sleep for a week. I let my eyes drift shut, only to be rustled awake.

"Take these first." Cole handed me the bottle of water and two little white pills. I arched my brow in expectation. "It's just some hospital grade Tylenol I had from my last gunshot wound three months ago."

"What, you randomly just carry drugs around?" I popped the pills in my mouth and took a swallow of water.

Cole rolled his eyes and took the bottle from me, putting it on the table next to the couch. "Whatever works."

"I really wanted a shower," I grumbled.

"And I really want to turn you over my knee and spank your ass for being so damn stubborn, but I won't. So get some rest, we'll talk in the morning," he replied gruffly.

"Yeah, that's fine." I pushed myself up, so I was sitting up. "We'll talk in the morning."

Cole groaned and ran his hand over his face. "What are you doing?"

I grabbed his hand and pulled myself up. The man may have been over a foot taller than me, but I glared at him anyway. "I'm taking a hot shower, then I'll put myself to bed." I walked gingerly toward the bathroom. His footsteps followed me down the small hall and into the primary bedroom and bathroom. While Maks was out gallivanting and doing his enforcer business with the Bratva, I found myself alone at home more often than not. I was bored, so I took to Youtube and Pinterest and figured out how to reno the house. I gutted the primary bathroom and turned it into my tropical oasis with a shower with multiple shower heads and a large bench. Maks used to joke it was a sex shower, but it was never used for that purpose.

Of course, the thought of having sex in my shower had my face feeling hot with blush, as I made my way into my oasis. I turned on the multiple heads. Cole leaned against the door frame, his eyebrow arched.

"What, Cole?"

"I'm waiting for you to ask for my help to get undressed." Cole smirked.

I scoffed. "You're going to be waiting awhile. I hit my head, but I'm not broken." I went to lift the grungy T-shirt off my body then paused. "Well? You can leave now."

Cole chuckled darkly. "I'm good with where I am."

I rolled my eyes and pulled the shirt over my head carefully. I winced at the pull in my shoulders. I would never admit this to him, but my body ached in ways I hadn't felt in a while.

"You have a few minutes before the meds kick in. If you're going to shower, you better do it now so I don't have to come in and save you from drowning." His low command sent shivers down my spine.

"Are you going to join me then?" I murmured, as I watched his reflection in the mirror. His tall, built frame filled my doorway. His thick biceps tested the fabric and stretch of his dark sleeves. Cole's messy hair was longer than I saw before, and I quite liked it. His eyes darkened as his gaze drifted up and down my body.

"I don't think so, kitten. Hurry up. The last thing I need you to do is fall again."

"It's freaking Tylenol. I think I'll be fine." I shucked off my shorts and ignored his muted groan when I turned around. I shimmied off my emerald-green thong and kicked it over toward the door. I stood in front of him, stark naked and unafraid of his smoked-whiskey eyes. My chin raised in a challenge as I opened the glass shower door and slid in. The steam enveloped me like a warm blanket, but it was his stare that heated me to my core.

I carefully tucked my hair into the cap then took my time washing every square inch of my body with my orange and vanilla body wash. My hand glazed down my stomach and brushed against my thighs, all while my eyes were glued to his. I didn't know what was going through my mind. Maybe it was the concussion. Maybe it was the buildup of stress and anxiety. But I just wanted to feel. I wanted to have his touch, his attention. Something. Something to make me feel more than what I was feeling right then. If we could have this one moment in time, I would never ask for anything ever again. I watched his jaw clenched as my fingers reached the apex of my thighs. Wetness gathered at my entrance, my pussy swollen with need.

"Cole. Please." The plea wasn't loud, but I knew he could hear me over the rushing water.

"Fuck it."

NINE

Cole

I PUSHED off the door frame. The kitten had shown me her tiny claws. But it was time to show her who was boss. I reached behind me and pulled off my shirt. I kicked off my boots and hurriedly slammed down my jeans, kicking them off. Need and desire tried to override any sense of anger or sensibility I had, but I kept myself in check. I let myself into the shower, and stood in front of her, and watched as her fingers traced what I wanted to taste. My body barely touched hers, but I could feel the heat emanating from her body.

The scent of orange and vanilla filled the room, but that wasn't even the best fragrance in the room. I could smell her arousal. My kitten needed to be tamed. My hand slowly reached up and grasped the base of her head, tilting her head back. I brought my face down to her five-three frame, and ran my nose under her jaw line, inhaling her scent. My mouth watered, and I wrapped my arms around her waist, jerking her to me. My cock, harder than a steel pipe, pressed against her stomach. My lips found hers. I wasn't gentle nor slow. I took what I wanted, what I needed, what she owed me.

"This isn't going to happen again," she muttered against my lips. I dug my fingers into her thick ass and held her tightly.

I chuckled darkly. "Sweetheart, like I'm letting you make any more decisions. You're mine. You've always been mine. Nothing you say or do will ever change that." I pressed her closer to me.

I swallowed her moan, my free hand tracing lightly down the side of her hips. She arched into me.

"Nah, kitten. As much as I want to take advantage of you tonight, I'm truly not an asshole. Let's get you cleaned up and in bed." She whined and pressed against my front. I swallowed my groan.

A sigh of frustration left her lips and I smiled. "I know, sweetness. I know. You don't know how badly I want to slide into you right now." I pressed my body into hers. "Fuck. I just want to slide so deep into you. So fucking badly. But you're hurt. I want to be able to bend you and play with you, keep you on fucking edge until you're on the verge of going crazy. But not today." My hands gripped her waist tightly as she let out a whimper.. "Let me take care of you." I took the loofah and dropped it onto the bench. I cupped the back of her head and pushed her back against the wall. My fingers left her waist and trailed down her outer thigh. Her skin pebbled, despite the steam and the hot water. Her thighs widened in anticipation; her eager breath hitched.

I let my hand drop and my fingers graze her inner thigh, trailing up to the heat at her apex. Her smooth skin felt like satin, as my touch danced around her clit, trailing on the edges of her outer lips. Her breath hitched and I smirked. She was already soaked for me, and it wasn't because of the shower. I sunk my first two fingers into her tight pussy, her muscles clutching them like a vice.

"You feel so good, kitten. So fucking tight," I moaned into her ear. The palm of my hand grinded against her clit as my fingers moved in a "come hither motion." Her breath exhaled in a whine as I stroked her most sensitive pressure point. My other hand grasped her heavy breast, rolling my thumb across her nipples, twisting and pulling lightly. Evie's jaw slacked and her eyes rolled back into her head as she rolled her hips into my touch. Fuck.

"You're so damn responsive," I murmured. My lips dropped down to her neck, sipping the drops from her hot skin.

It wouldn't take long for her to come and damn if I didn't want to inhale every fucking breath she took. My cock twitched, demanding I sheath myself into her heat. I wanted to. Need coursed through me. But I knew I had to be patient.

"I want to touch you." The plea in her voice caused my cock to leak precum. The feel of her slippery hands encasing my dick was almost my undoing. She stroked me with even, hard pressure from the base to the tip. The sounds of our mixed groans and moans filled the shower. Her fingers teased each stud of my Jacob's ladder piercings. I groaned, my forehead buried into her neck. My fingers thrusted inside her heat, in time with her strokes. One of her hands grazed up my neck and locked onto my hair, tugging hard. My balls tightened and spine tingled as she forced my head up and slammed her lips onto mine. Our tongues clashed for dominance in a hot and sloppy wet kiss. I increased the pressure on her clit with my thumb and felt her inner walls flutter around my fingers.

"Fuck, Evie. Come for me," I groaned. Her hands worked my dick faster and a high-pitched groan escaped her mouth. Evie's pussy pulsed as she gushed around my hand, her cries loud and echoing in the room. Heat shot through my body as I sprayed her belly with my cum. My mouth went to her neck and bit down, not enough to break skin but hard enough to leave a mark. My mark. Her hands kept working, milking me, and prolonging my orgasm.

Our breath mingled as we panted heavily. I nipped her lips and slowly retracted my fingers from her pussy's vice. Her heavy-lidded gaze watched as I sucked her deliciousness off my fingers. I pressed my forehead to hers.

"You're fucking breathtaking, kitten. I can't wait to do this every night," I murmured to my wife. She pressed her lips to mine. It was a kiss that was slower, but more intense than the one we had just shared. Knowing the pills I gave her was going to be kicking soon, I wrapped my arm around her waist and turned her under the shower. I gently washed my release from her skin, begrudgingly. She dropped her head, her head resting on my chest. Languid and sated, exactly how I wanted her.

"Let's get you to bed, kitten." I quickly washed myself, using her sweet-orange scented body wash, then turned off the water. I grabbed a towel from the hook and patted her dry before roughly toweling myself off. After taking off her shower cap and helping her put on her bonnet, I followed her over to the bed and pulled back her deep purple duvet and sheets.

"How are you feeling, kitten?" I murmured, as I tucked her in.

"I'm feeling better. I'm totally conscious but the pain is gone," she replied sleepily.

"Good." I kissed her temple.

"Stay. I want you to stay." Her barely there whisper tugged at my heart. I could have blamed the drug, but sometimes the sober words come out when the person is anything but. She wanted me to stay. I smirked.

"I wouldn't fucking dream of leaving." She smiled as she faded out. I watched as sleep overtook her, then moved over to my bag I brought with me. After Charlie was kidnapped, Sketch made sure there was a way he'd never lose track of her again. And of course, since I found my wife again after all those years, I made sure to have a way as well.

I slipped the hollowed tip syringe out of its packaging. Zeke tore into me when I first asked Sketch about it, but Sketch, the maniacal mother fucker that he was, just gave a me a grin and threw me the box. The tracker was pre-loaded and the app was already downloaded to my phone. Sometimes kittens get skittish, and they run away. I needed to make sure she didn't get too far.

I crept back to my sleeping beauty laying on her side. Her naked skin beckoned for my touch, and I resisted the urge to climb into bed. I swabbed her shoulder with the alcohol wipe and slipped in the needle. Evie's body flinched as I pushed in the plunger, but there was no other reaction. Sighing in relief, I wiped away the minimal drops of blood and disposed of the needle and case into my bag. I slid into bed and pulled her into my arms. I didn't plan on telling her and I hoped I'd never have to. Because if I did, it would have meant I failed in protecting her.

TEN

Cole

I woke gradually, feeling warm. Content. I laid on my side, my body curved around Evie's. Her warm skin was bare against mine. My woman. My wife. I never wanted this feeling to end. My hard dick throbbed in between her ass cheeks. My lips found her neck, my hips thrusted slightly to find the friction.

A low moan escaped her lips. I could see her eyes were still shut. My hand was resting protectively on her stomach slid lower. My fingers traced her bare skin, to the wet heat of her center.

"Fuck, baby." I groaned softly into the crook of her neck. Her ass pushed into my pelvis, grinding into me.

"Cole," she breathed.

"Baby, you're hurt," I whispered, my lips caressing her ear. My thrusts became more urgent. Fuck, I needed to get inside her.

. . .

"PLEASE." The breathy moan was my undoing. I wiggled my body lower down the mattress, before lifting her leg. Thank fuck we went to bed naked. Although, I doubt any material could have kept us apart. I slid into her soaked pussy, my cock immediately gripped in her vice-like inner walls.

"YOU'RE SO ready for me, kitten." Thrust. "God damn, you feel like fucking heaven." Thrust. I tried to keep my movements gentle but need quickly overtook any rational thought. My fingers rolled around her clit as she rocked her body against mine. Her fast pants of breath and the quivering of her inner walls told me she was close. Evie widened her leg and brought it over my hip, allowing me greater access. I plunged deeper, my piercings dragging against her G-spot.

"COLE. God—I'm going to come. Please god, let me come." The breathless plea snapped any resemblance of control I had. My thrusts quickened; my pelvis slapped at her ass. My fingers continued to rub her clit and her core tightened around me. Pressure built at my spine.

"COME ON MY BIG COCK, Evie. Come now!" I roared. She came with a shudder, as her cum soaked my cock. I continued my assault, plunging in as dep as I could, before I erupted inside her drenched pussy.

My breath heaving, I burrowed my face into Evie's neck. I didn't want to move, but I knew I needed to. I moved her leg off me, then slowly withdrew. My body protested, not wanting to leave her heat, but I knew it was time to wake up.

I made my way to the bathroom, cleaned myself up, then

wet a washcloth in hot water. I made my way back to the bed and gently cleaned her off, before climbing back into the bed. I wasn't ready to face the real world just yet.

I LAID ON MY BACK, with Evie's body curved around me. I tightened my arm around her and pressed my lips to her forehead. After morning's, I knew everything had changed. We both knew it. Whether she wanted it to or not, we were in this shit together. And I wasn't about to let the fucking Syndicate say otherwise. She reached her around across my chest and pressed her lips against my pec.

"Good morning, beauty." I murmured.

She buried her face into my chest. "Mmmph"

"Still not a morning bird?" I chuckled quietly. We needed to talk soon and I knew it would pop this cozy bubble we were in. I needed to keep it together before everything changed.

"I work mids and nights. Your mornings are my bedtimes. But keep waking me up like that, and I could probably change my mind," she mumbled. Her arm reached across my waist, and she nestled closer. My kitten was a snuggler in the morning. I smiled as I tucked this information away, knowing full well if I said anything, she would pull away.

"How's your head?" I murmured.

Evie reached up, brushing aside her bonnet, and ran her finger gently over the gash on her forehead. "It hurts, but nothing more than a mild headache."

I leaned back and lifted her chin. "Look at me, beauty." My eyes roamed over her face. A bump had already formed on her cheek, marring her silky skin. Her honey eyes were alert, framed by beautiful thick lashes. Her fuller bottom lip tempted me, and I gently brushed my thumb across it. "Seriously? Are you okay? Do you want me to take you to get checked out?"

Her eyes fluttered closed and her pink tongue darted out to catch my thumb. A low groan escaped, and I closed my eyes. My cock twitched under the sheet, already ready to find home again. This morning is what I had been dreaming of. I couldn't think of a better way to wake up than to sink my cock into her warm ...

Pain shot through my groin as a bowling ball landed on my crotch, and I closed my eyes in agony.

"Fuck." My body bowed under the pressure and my arm darted out, hoping to dislodge whatever had dropped on me. Sharp pinpricks dug their way into my skin and a high-pitched yelp came out.

"Mario! No!" Evie's voice cried out. The weight disappeared off my groin, and I opened my eyes.

"Who the fuck is Mario?" I gasped out.

"Oh my god, are you okay?" Evie asked, sitting up. The deep purple bed sheet dropped from her chest, and I was momentarily distracted by the sight of her gorgeous breasts with dusky brown nipples. Despite the pain I was in, my cock twitched again.

"I forgot to warn you about him. Mario is my cat," Evie said, hiding her smile. I glared at her with narrow eyes.

"You forgot to mention you have a sadist as a companion?" The pain had subsided to a low throb. Evie just smiled and flipped her hair out of her face.

"You didn't notice him last night?"

"I think I would have noticed a murderous feline in the house," I snarked back.

"You're in his spot." I glanced to the right of me. The black and white bowling ball laid on his side, licking his paw while his green eyes stared at me.

"You know cats steal people's souls right? And does he have extra thumbs?" My mouth gaped open at the black and white marshmallow with paws stared at me with slanted eyes. I could tell the furry bastard was planning my demise. I never thought I'd see my end at the paws of a murderous feline.

Evie rolled her eyes, and my palms itched to smack her ass in punishment. "He does not steal people's souls. But if you leave your french fries alone for a minute, he'll steal those. And yes, he has extra toes on each paw. He's polydactyl. You know, like Hemmingway's cats." My blank stare caused her to snort in laughter. "Okay, Ernest Hemingway... You know? The famous author? He had a bunch of these types of cats around his place in Key West. It's a thing." She shook her head at my ignorance.

"Cats with thumbs will try and take over the world. You better watch yourself," I snarked dryly. Although with the way the fucker was looking at me, I shouldn't have joked. She giggled but then sighed once she caught my eye.

She leaned against her dark gray upholstered headboard. "I guess we need to have the talk."

I mimicked her pose. "Yeah, I think we do. I'm trying to control my emotions here, but I need some clarity on what the hell happened."

Evie looked down at her hands in defeat. "I think you know pretty much everything."

I nodded. "I do. But I need to hear from you. Give me everything. Let's start with the basics. Who the hell are you?"

"You know I don't know much about you either, right?" She shot back. I just grinned back. My girl was feeling feisty, and I was here for it

I nodded. "Right. But I am not involved with a dangerous crime syndicate. You are. So..." I gestured around.

She rolled her eyes and sighed. "Fine. My name is Evelyn Rosa Banks, daughter of Andres and Isla Banks. I was born September seventeenth in Chicago. My father is Afro-Mexican, my mother is Black. I'm a Virgo, love smutty romance novels, and cats. I hate to cook, I eat way too much ice cream, and I'm scared of spiders. Anything else you want to know?" she sassed. "Now it's your turn."

"Special Operations Officer, Cole Michael Parker. I'm a Valentine's baby and I have no clue what sign I am. I was born and raised in Baltimore. I have two sisters, a whole bunch of brothers from other mothers, and a pittie-mix named Jax, who is the best boy. I like blowing things up, riding dirt bikes, and dogs. I have a massive sweet tooth, but my favorite meal is definitely you," I replied, eyeing her up and down.

She shoved my shoulder. "Okay, Casanova." She paused. "What are you doing here?"

"Nyuah. It's my turn to ask the question." I paused, my eyes running over her face. I saw trepidation in her eyes and while I knew this whole thing sucked, I needed her to be honest with me.

"Tell me about Mexico. Was any of that real?" I dropped the act, and let the vulnerability come through. Out of all the questions I had for her, this was the one I needed the most answers to.

Evie was silent for a beat and played with her fingernails, chipping off the lavender paint. I placed my hands over hers, begging silently for her to look up at me. She finally did, and sadness was in her eyes.

"It was as real as it could be at eighteen. We only knew each other for what? Ten days?" she replied quietly. "Did I want it to be real? Of course I did. You made me feel so much more than I thought I could. You made me feel loved, cherished, and like a human with a choice. I don't know what I was looking for when I met you on the beach, but for the briefest moment, I felt so alive."

I glared at her with narrowed eyes. "Why did you leave me in Mexico? Why didn't you tell me what was going on? I could have helped you get away from there." My heart felt like it was breaking all over again.

Evie chuckled darkly. "I was young but not stupid, Cole. I knew better than to go against my father and the Bratva."

"So why even do it? Why spend all that time with me? Was I something to do before you got hitched to your Russian husband?" I snapped.

"Do you think I wanted to hide that from you?" she exclaimed, her hands flying. "You were the first man, the only man, who has made me feel the way you did. I wanted to tell you. I hated lying to you. But if I told you the truth it would have put you in even more danger."

"But you could have fucking told me!" I threw up my hands in exasperation.

She argued. "What would I have said, Cole? That I was in an arranged marriage with someone from the Russian Bratva? For the first time ever, I was living my own life and going by my own rules? That for the first time in my life, I felt safe and comforted? You were the only person I had a real connection with, other than my abuela. Forgive me for wanting to linger in the fantasy for a little bit."

"Your little game broke my fucking heart! If you would have said you were fucking engaged, I would have stayed away from you. I wouldn't have spent all that time with you. I wouldn't have given up my leave and risked AWOL. And I sure as hell wouldn't have said those vows in the church!" I shouted. I got up and paced the room. Anger fired within me. At the very bottom of my heart, I could understand what happened. But she broke me. I gave my heart to her and she's held it for so fucking long, I haven't been able to move on.

Hurt crossed over her face briefly before a mask slid into place. "Then why are you back, Cole? If I did so much damage to you, why the hell are you here with me? Why don't you leave me the hell alone?" She snapped coldly.

My retort was rudely interrupted when a loud knock echoed through the small house. Evie's black hair whipped around as her eyes met mine in fear. I quickly tugged on the sweatpants I had left on the floor and grabbed my Glock while Evie dressed. She pulled a worn, purple robe around her night shirt and glared at me.

"Stay here," she ordered, as she rushed to the door. I crept behind the cracked open bedroom door, peering through the gap. The knocks came harder, and she paused right before the door. She took a deep breath, then opened the door wide enough to peek out.

"What the hell took you so long?" A loud male voice I didn't recognize came through the front door.

"What do you need, Julian?" Evie's spine stiffened and she crossed her arms.

"I heard shouting. Who's in there with you? You finally got a new man?" The smarminess pulled at my gut and there's nothing more I wanted than to knock this full on his ass.

"I was listening to an audiobook. What do you need?" Evie demanded through gritted teeth.

"I was just trying to see if you were good. I heard about the bar last night." The voice had my teeth grinding, as well. I angled my body more to see.

Evie sighed. "I really don't have much to say about it because I don't know much. Is that all you needed?"

"You look tired, Evie. How about I come and help you settle—" Evie placed her hand on the door to close it. A growl came from deep inside me. The thought of another man in this house had my blood boiling. I counted the ways I could hang this man by his testicles while she continued her conversation.

"No." Evie's voice grew cold.

"I know you're good, but I'm sure I could make you feel better. Make you some tea, or maybe rub your back?" The lecherous tone snapped my last nerve. I edged the door that was blocking my view out of the way. If the bastard took one foot through the doorway, I could get a shot. It wouldn't be clean - but at this point, I didn't really care.

"Absolutely not. I don't need your help. I don't want your help. And for fuck's sake, I don't want you. Now unless you have something important to tell me, you need to leave." Evie snapped. Her patience, and mine, were hanging on by a thread.

"Aye! Okay okay. Keep your panties on, Evie. I was just being friendly and making sure my friend is okay. Especially after a crazy night like last night." I could see directly down the hall to the front door, but I couldn't see the joker who thought he had a chance with my wife.

"Why do you keep bringing it up? What did you hear about last night?" Evie asked sharply.

A pregnant pause, I could tell whoever she was talking to, was suddenly uncomfortable by his stuttering.

"I just heard there was a commotion. I tried to go check it out, but we couldn't get close." The voice stammered, suddenly becoming uncomfortable.

"Who is we?"

"Oh, I mean me. I was with Toby, and we thought we could help..."

"For the love of fucking god, Julian. How many times do I have to tell you? You don't need to be trying to get in with Sebastian's crew." Evie threw up her arms in frustration and her robe fell open. A growl came low in my chest as she quickly pulled it back together. I wanted to rip this dude's eyes out of his socket for seeing what's mine.

"I mean, we're not trying to get..." Julian's voice stammered but Evie threw up her hand to stop him.

"If you keep playing these damn stupid games, you're going to win the stupid prizes. You're smart, Julian. Use your damn head. This isn't the crew you want to get in with. I don't know what else to tell you." She put her hand back on the door, as if to close it.

"Yeah. Well. We'll see. Either way, Big Boss man wants you to come in this afternoon."

"Why didn't he text me?" Suddenly Evie's hand covered her face. "I must have left the phone in my car. It was in my purse. Which is probably toast right now."

"Probably. Anyway, he wanted me to give you this and to tell you to be at the spot at two o'clock." I saw a black phone being smacked in Evie's hand. "I guess since you don't have a car, I could come and pick you up?" The interest coming from the asshole annoyed the fuck out of me and I wanted to knock the bastard out.

"I'll figure out a ride. Thanks Julian." Evie quickly shut the door and locked the deadbolt. She tugged her robe closed and came down the hall with the phone in her hand, her finger over her lips to stop me from saying anything. I understood, the likelihood the phone was bugged and already active was high. She moved through her room and into her closet, where she took out a metal looking box. I looked at her with suspicion, as she placed the phone into the box, then shut the lid and put it toward the back of her shelf.

"It's a Zeke special, isn't it?" I recognized his design immediately. Whenever we traveled, we always carried a military grade case which prevented anyone from hacking into our phones or laptops by blocking any signal in or out of the box. The contraption was the first idea Zeke created that made him millions.

Evie gave me a grim smile, worry crinkled in her eyes. "Yep. The day after he found me through Brittny and the Rainbow

Trail, this was mailed to me through my favorite bookstore. This along with a phone, and a sweeping tool that checks for cameras and microphones. The man's thorough for sure."

I grabbed her waist and pulled her into me, loving as she instinctively sank into me. I buried my face into her neck. "I'm sorry." I murmured.

"Me too." Her soft sigh fractured my heart.

"I hate that you're in this situation." I paused. "I hate even more that we're in this situation."

She wrapped her arms around my neck. "I know. I do too. But I feel like we're coming up to the end. There is this vibe in the shop, like they're expecting something big to happen. People are on edge." Her teeth tugged on her bottom lip.

"All the more reason to bounce out now. Tell them you're going to see your Abuelita," I suggested.

She pulled out of my arms, and I felt the cold of the loss immediately. She went over to her dresser and pulled out some clothes. "I don't know how to give you the answer that will placate your fears or satisfy your worries," she replied dryly as she pulled on a long sleeve black tee and a pair of gray wide legged dress pants with a belt,

"You don't have to do this."

"I have a job to do, Cole," she muttered. She went into the ensuite bathroom and started pulling out products onto the counter. She hung up her bonnet and set about doing her skin care routine.

"Come home with me. This isn't your fight anymore. Let us take care of this," I tried again but the stubborn woman ignored me for a moment. I leaned against the door frame and crossed my arms.

"It's time for you to leave," she said flatly, staring at me through the mirror.

"Nah, kitten. I told you last night, you're not getting away from me that easily." I walked up behind her and wrapped my arms around her waist, nuzzling my face in her neck. For a moment, she relaxed into me. But quickly stiffened.

"And I told you I have a life here." She put the lid back onto the pot of lotion she was using and slammed it down to the counter.

"You have a life? What kind of fucking life is? A life of a widow who is pandering to an organized crime syndicate, trafficking women and children? That's no fucking life, Evie," I snapped.

"It's my fucking life!" She turned and pushed me away. Not expecting it, I stepped back. "I'm doing what I need to do in order to survive. I'm doing what I need to do to save the lives of innocents. For fuck's sake Cole, you put your life on the line for the same people. Why not me? Why am I getting called out for it?"

"It's completely different and you know it. I'm a damn professional. You're not. I've had years of intense training. You have not. I have the Alpha team behind me. You have no one to support you or have your back."

Rage flared in her eyes, and I knew I took it too far. This fucking woman. She drove me to the brink of insanity with her damn stubbornness.

"Fuck you, Cole. You have no idea how capable I am. You have no idea what I have gone through or what I have done to get to this point. This is my life; my fucking redemption and I'm going to see it through." She pushed me away even more and stormed back into her bedroom. "It's time for you to leave."

"Kitten..."

"No Cole. You don't get to call me terms of endearment if you're also going to criticize me at the same time. It doesn't work like that." She turned away from me with her eyes blazed in emotions. Shit. I knew I hurt her, but I couldn't stop the words from coming out. My primal focus was her safety, first and foremost.

"Fuck! Kitten, listen. At least let me put some cameras —" I tried to placate her reaction, but I got cut off with a slice through the air

"You think I don't have cameras already? Am I such a novice to you that you think I've been nonchalant about my security? I've been doing this for ten years. I grew up in this life. I know what I'm doing, so go fuck yourself out of my house. Now!" she seethed. Fire flicked through my body. Anger looked beautiful on her. The brief interlude we had earlier seemed like a distant memory, and damned if I didn't want to feel her body against mine. But I feared for my life if I made such a move. I knew I was a dick for saying that to her.

"Then I need you to do me a favor and take these." I reached into my pocket and pulled out four small, circular discs in a tiny plastic baggie. "They're bugs. Put them wherever you can. It'll help us listen in."

Irritation came over her beautiful features. "These are undetectable. You won't get caught. I promise," I soothed, thinking she was unsure about her safety. I would never do anything I would think would cause her more trouble. I trusted Zeke's devices more than I trusted most developers. When he said they were undetectable, they were.

She rolled her eyes. "Trust me. I know. They sweep the damn place every day and monitor everything coming in and going out. Zeke already sent me some. But I'll take a few more," she said dryly, and shoved the baggie into her pocket.

"He already sent them?" I swore. Why did it seem like I was being anything but helpful? Zeke had already had her on a good path forward.

"You seriously underestimate me. First, you didn't think I knew what I was doing, and now you're giving me something to plant to help you? Please make up your mind." She shrugged me off in anger.

I moved slowly to her and cupped her face. I pressed my forehead against hers. "I'm sorry. I was wrong. I know you're more than capable and I know you know what you're doing. But the fact I have to let you out of my sight has my monster in a rage right now and I hate it." I pressed my lips to hers, gently. "I'm going to go, but only because you need to go to work. How are you getting to the bar?"

Her lips pressed together in a thin line. "I'll call Jimmy." She turned back to the mirror and started brushing out her wavy locks.

My upper lip curled up in a snarl. "He wants to get into your pants."

Evie scoffed. "And you don't? Seriously? Just stop."

"Stop what?"

She ignored my question, and I grasped her chin firmly, not hard enough to hurt her but hard enough for her to turn back to me.

"Stop. What?" I demanded, as I stared into her beautiful honey eyes.

"Stop acting like you have any say in what I do. Stop acting like sex isn't all you want," she muttered. She pulled away and swiped some stuff onto her already long lashes. She didn't need anything more, as she was already so beautiful. But her beauty was already trying my patience.

"Honey, if you think I'm here just for the pussy, then I've been doing a shit job trying to explain myself to you," I snapped.

"Why are you here, Cole? Aside from taking down the Syndicate. Why the fuck are you here?" she demanded, pointing a finger in my chest.

I threw my hands up in exasperation. "Am I going insane?

Have you not been listening to me or are you stuck in your own fucking head!"

"Explain it to me like I'm a kid, Cole. Because the only thing I've heard from you, aside from telling me how to run this operation, is that I broke your heart. If I broke your heart so damn badly, then I *apologize*. I am sorry for running away from you in Mexico. I'm sorry my life wouldn't allow me to live the life I wanted to live with you. I'm sorry I broke your heart. Now. *There*. Are we good? *You can leave now*."

Evie slammed everything back into a drawer and brushed past me and moved into the kitchen. Mario's yowls for food increased loudly as I followed her. I pulled my T-shirt over my head and sniffed.

"What the hell is that smell?" My nose wrinkled in disgust.

"Mario doesn't like assholes." Evie smirked.

"He pissed on my shirt?" This fucking bastard of a cat. I glared at him, as he innocently licked his nuts. "I'm going to turn you into a pair of slippers" I grumbled as I plotted the black and white feline's demise as I yanked off the offending shirt and tossed it in the garbage can. I didn't have anything else with me, but I would be damned if I was driving around all day and smelling this foul.

Evie rolled her eyes and walked out of the room, only coming back with a black hoodie. She handed it to me with a smile.

I looked at it with suspicion. She looked entirely too happy for me to take it.

"What is up with the shirt?"

"Just in case you didn't want a cat-pee shirt, you can wear this. You're lucky I like my hoodies very oversized".

I took the shirt from her and unfolded it. The front of the sweatshirt had hot pink lettering which read "Tell me I'm a good girl", but the back had me gawking. In the same font, it said "But smack my ass and pull my hair first." My cock thickened instantly, and I growled. I grabbed her hand and pulled her against my body. Her body was pliant against mine, and she could tell how she affected me. I wretched her arm behind her tightly with one hand and with the other, grasped her hair at the base of her neck.

"Is this what you want, kitten? For me to tell you you're a good girl?" My lips chased her jawline and down her throat.

"I mean, every girl wants to be praised," she murmured breathlessly. She was just as affected, and god damn if I didn't love how responsive she was.

"You mean, you want me to tell you how good you felt next to me last night? About how this morning felt like heaven sliding into your tight cunt, feeling your slick heat surrounding my dick? Should I tell you how many times I have jerked off to the memories of not only Nashville, but of Sayulita as well? That night in the church was ten years ago but it was the best night of my life."

"Cole," she breathed. I placed my hands under her luscious ass cheeks and lifted her up. Her legs went around mine immediately, and I walked us over to the wall. I pressed my cock at the seam of her jeans. She shamelessly ground against me. I reached between us to the button of her pants when another knock came at the door.

"Fucking hell," I hissed. I dropped her legs and pressed my forehead to hers.

"You need to go, Cole," she said. Her smile was weary. "I can't pay attention to you while I'm trying to focus on this. I need to bring them down. I deserve to bring them down."

Another knock came, louder, and followed by a male voice. "Evie?"

I pulled back, my eyebrow raised and ignored whoever was at the door. "This shit again? What's it going to take for you to understand, kitten. I'm fucking helping you with this. I'm not going anywhere." I growled. My gripped around her waist tightened.

"If they find you, you're dead. If they know we have history, we're both dead." She gestured between us. "I'm not playing around. We're over."

"You're only putting off the inevitable, Evie."

Another knock came louder, and Evie pushed me away. "I mean it, Cole. We're done. Don't come back."

Molten hot anger furled through my veins, and I snarled at the thought of any alternative.

"You're letting them fucking win. And I won't tolerate that shit. I told you I won't let you go, and that's a hard truth. You're fucking mine." I kissed her full lips one more time, then slipped out the back door.

ELEVEN

Evie

I WATCHED Cole leave with a sigh. I didn't want to do it, to push him away yet again. But I knew it was for the best. I hurried over to the front door, only to see Jimmy waiting for me.

"I figured you needed a ride," he said with a grim smile.

"You figured right. Just give me a few minutes." I closed the door again and hurried back to my bathroom. Any summons from Sebastian was never a good sign and it could only mean we were hosting guests. I slid my feet into a pair of black slip-on Sketchers and checked my makeup. I pulled my hair back into a low ponytail. I was due for a hair appointment and quickly calculated the timing I had left. Depending on whatever Sebastian had me doing, I could possibly reach out to my girl in the next town over. But knowing him, it was not likely to happen. I grabbed a bottle of water, a bottle of acetaminophen, and a granola bar, then rushed out to meet Jimmy in the car.

"Do you know what's going on?" I asked, as I ripped open the granola bar. I took a large bite and looked at him expectantly. Jimmy winced and fidgeted in his seat.

"Tell me Jimmy. What kind of shitshow am I walking into?" I demanded.

Jimmy let out a huge exhale, and my stomach dropped. "Ma, I honestly don't know. I was called to the spot three hours ago. Everything there is in chaos right now. Apparently, there was a drop on one of the latest transports, so shit has hit the fan. Sebastian is calling for a tribunal with Dmitri on the seat."

A tribunal. Essentially a court with Sebastian as the judge, jury and executioner. That never boded well for whomever was being set up. The rest of the Syndicate world bear witness to whatever fuckery he had in store.

"Who is he bringing to the floor?" I replied nonchalantly. I crumbled up the granola bar wrapper and shoved it in the door cup holder. He side-eyed my mess, and I just batted my eyelashes.

Jimmy shook his head as he pulled up to a red light. "I have no clue. You know how these folks are paranoid. Some people are fussing because of the new product line, about how their cuts are being diminished because of the new way Sebastian is doing business. They can't stop whining. Oh, and get this shit. There have been whispers of a mole, but I have no clue how. It's not like he doesn't monitor all communications coming in and out of the building. They just did a sweep, and there wasn't anything for him to find there."

My heart raced. Any thought of a potential mole could bring unwanted attention to me, and that's not something I needed to happen. I kept my facade calm, but inwardly I panicked.

Jimmy rolled his eyes. "Do you want your diabetes now or later?" He quipped. I scoffed at his innocent question.

"Since when is that even a question? Now of course," I scoffed.

We took a run through a local coffee drive-thru, where I ordered my usual quad-shot caramel latte and peanut butter scone.

"Does it come with a side of insulin?" Jimmy quipped.

"Shut up and just drive." I took a bite of the moist, peanut buttery goodness and almost let out a moan. It was so damn good. If I was going to go in front of a firing squad, I was going to go out all buzzed up on sugar.

It didn't take long before we pulled up to the bar, the remnants of yesterday's shooting barely visible. Unless you were specifically looking for bullet fragments in the trees. I expected to see burned out remains of my car, it was gone. There was barely a burned ring around the spot where my SUV previously sat.

The peanut butter scone sat heavily in my stomach as I stared at the set of buildings in front of me. I heaved a deep breath and pushed open the door. Jimmy had already reached the entrance before I made two steps forward. Thanks for leaving me to the firing squad. I reached into my pocket and made sure the baggie of bugs was still hidden, then heaved a quick prayer to whoever was listening up above to protect me and I headed up the brick stairs. Thankfully, my days of being searched were long gone, but the very thought of them going through my pockets made my heart race in fear.

I walked into the dark room. Roger was the sole person in the room, and he looked bored as he flipped through the newspaper. I raised my eyebrow in question, and he nodded his head toward the back. He was one of the original bartenders from when we first moved out here five years ago. It's safe to say he's seen some shit go down. Dmitri kept him around because he didn't say anything and he was loyal.

Roger, the ever-stoic grump ass, just shrugged. "I was told there's a stack of work on your desk. I'm here, keeping watch." I internally rolled my eyes. Thanks for nothing, jerk. I could only imagine what the paperwork would be.

I grabbed a bottle of my favorite bottle of maple bourbon cream and marched back into the office. I needed something to get through this, and my favorite distillery was a must. After heaving a huge sigh and a shot of bourbon, I got to work. I flicked through the papers on my desk, my stomach churning at the sight of how many children were included on this ship-ment. Newly teens, babies, and even teenage mothers. I wanted to crawl out of my own skin and burn the world fucking down.

Fuck. I picked up my encrypted phone and dialed my first customer on the list.

"Duyduğuma göre ince yıllanmış bir şişe burbon arıyor-muşsun. Siz de bir şişe votka ile ilgileniyor musunuz?" I croon into the phone, asking the Turkish client what they would be interested in. Our code was pretty straight forward but seeing as how I was calling from a distillery, using forms of alcohol as code words for the types of products we sell.

"Votka kaç yillik?"

My stomach churned and bile crept up my throat. I digested the Turkish man's question on age. I answered as vaguely as I could and waited for his confirmation. Then I got to make several calls similar to the last. Korean, Arabic. Urdu. Russian. And plenty of English. Once I finished my list, I immediately ran for the bathroom and threw up what little I had left in my stomach. I couldn't do this anymore. I couldn't deal with the potential of children being hurt. It was time to call this in. I was done. And knowing that Cole was here waiting for me, helped me solidify my position.

I had already given Zeke and company the back door to my computer. As long as I kept it on and running, they could see everything and anything that went through. I kept notes on everything. Names. Shipment dates. Transaction history. And even bank accounts and wire transfers. It was time to put my exit plan into action. There was one more step I needed to take.

I made my way back into the main bar area.

"Are they still down there?" I asked, pouring myself a ginger ale. I kept myself calm, and unnerved, despite my blood raging. I took a sip of the bubbles and urged my nausea to settle.

Roger grunted in confirmation. Ever the great communicator, I thought dryly. "You're being beckoned." He mumbled, then nodded again at the door.

My head twisted over to him, and I frowned. "Did they want me to go down there?" A bit of confusion and fear rose in me. Fuck. There was no reason for me to be there. My business was always conducted via electronic means, there was never a need for face to face transactions with any of these monsters.

Roger shrugged, his beady brown eyes never leaving his newspaper. Fucking hell. I grabbed my glass of soda and raised it in a fake salute to him. "Thanks, Roger."

I fingered the devices in my pocket. I placed three so far, one under my keyboard and two in the bar area. Thanks to Zeke, I had already planted five of them throughout the facility. But I had yet to venture out to where it would be the most beneficial. Where all the leaders gathered. And while I didn't plan on being seen, being beckoned down there helped with any cover story I needed in order to drop the last devices. I headed toward the cellar. The tunnels that ran between all of the buildings also went to the barn behind our bar. It was once a former meat processing plant. Under the guise of a bourbon distillery called CS Brewery, Maks retrofitted the massive barn with a proper sewage, electricity, and water system. Theoretically, it could be used as a distillery, for our own brand of whiskey we were "making". But in reality, it was used as the

Syndicate's primary storage location for our products before the transfer. A place well hidden from any street unless you were really looking and it gave a great reason why the semi-trucks would come through periodically.

As I made my way through the narrow concrete tunnels, I could hear the noise coming from up ahead. I could only imagine what awaited me. Maybe Sebastian torturing some poor woman, who the hell knew.

I moved through the musty, dank cellar. The sole yellow-white light bulb hung loosely from the ceiling, casting shadows along the shelves and corners. I knew very little about the history of our buildings. But I presumed the secrets laid within these walls were those which shouldn't be shared. Bootlegging was a dangerous business, and I was sure this building had seen more than its fair share of blood and death.

I stopped before I got to the doorway, shielded by the shadows and surveyed the room before me. Leaders from various Syndicate organizations filled the room, seating in a circle of chairs. In the middle of the circle, Sebastian stood on a dais, his dark brown eyes surveying his crowd. A square cage hung over him, shaking. Soft whimpers and moans came from above. I grimaced at the sight of a woman, hogtied with a masking tape covering her mouth. I could only imagine what they had planned for her.

If there was ever a time for a listening device, it was now. I shoved my hand into my pocket and grabbed the last small black disc. I knew there were cameras in the corridors, so I kept my back to the corridor as I leaned against the doorframe. Acting as if I had an itch, I nonchalantly let the disc fall to my feet as I scratched my arm. I prayed to whoever was listening that they would watch over me, because I sure as hell didn't know what I was getting into.

"Gentleman! Let's get started," Sebastian called out, his

deep voice echoing. I jumped at the sound of his voice, his tall frame towering over everyone. Dressed in a dark suit and shirt, he fitted the image of a drug cartel kingpin. Tattoos ran across his bald head and neck. Thick gold chains hung over his black dress shirt. I looked at him with a critical eye. Of all the Syndicate members, he was the one I feared the most. He had the role of the leader, and the backing of both the Bratva and Cruz Cartels. He had little to fear by way of repercussions.

"I welcome you all here tonight in our humble enclave. I have called this meeting of the leaders to not only continue to go over our plans for the future but also talk about how to move forward in this ever-changing landscape. Our businesses have been successful, but I know we're only on the cusp of greatness. However, we have to understand not everyone wants to see us succeed." He gestured to his left, where Dmitri sat. Even from my distance, I could see sweat beaded on his brow. What the hell is going on?

"We were fortunate to have met Dmitri and the Alexyandez Bratva several years ago. Through many transactions, we have developed a model plan which not only paves the way for future business endeavors, but also for many years with a family alliance. A family alliance that has the Syndicate taking steps into a new realm of possibilities. We must stay ahead of our competition in order to bring them to their knees."

I couldn't comprehend what he was talking about. What family alliance? The only way for families to become aligned was to...

"Evelyn Rose Banks-Alexyandez." My name from his lips froze my heart as I glanced up in shock. "I wish to introduce you to the world in which you've helped cultivate." Sebastian beckoned me toward the dais. My heart stammered as my pulse quickened. A noise rustled behind me, and I peeked over my shoulder to find a large man, with long blond hair, wearing a suit. I knew without looking the man had enough fire power to run through me if I made a misstep. I would barely make it to the end of the hall before I died. The behemoth nodded for me to move forward. My steps stuttered as I made my way to the front, slowly. It felt both forever and too quick. Once I reached him, Sebastian grabbed my wrist and pulled me up onto the stage with him. The eyes of a dozen men, lecherous and evil, felt like a hot fire on my skin. Inside, I so badly wanted to scream in terror. But I refused to let them see. My spine stiffened, and I raised my chin to them in defiance.

"That's right. Like a queen, show them who rules you," Sebastian murmured as his eyes raked up and down my body. He kept hold of my wrist and turned me to face the crowd.

"You may know her as the daughter of the Banker. You may also know of her other moniker, the Broker. But soon, Evie will have another title."

My stomach dropped as Sebastian looked down at me and an evil grin appeared on his face.

"My wife."

TWELVE

Cole

I put the phone next to my ear as I hustled through the woods behind Evie's house, to where I parked my truck two blocks away. Anger fueled my speed. I was mad at the world; particularly how stubborn Evie was.

"I was just about to call you." Zeke's voice came through.

"You need me?" I snapped, as I pulled away from the curb and headed north. I needed food, a shower, and some answers. It didn't matter in which order.

"Yeah. Shit's going down."

The hair on the back of my neck stood up. "What's going on?"

"Can't talk on open channels. Get back to your laptop and log on. I think you need to see this." He hung up and all thoughts of food went out the window. I did a U-turn in the middle of the road and sped toward my hotel.

I could only image the fuckery Zeke found. I pulled into the parking spot in front of my door and quickly made my way inside. I grabbed my laptop from my bag and booted it up. Knowing it would take at least five minutes before it was ready, I jumped into the shower. I hated washing off her scent but I knew I needed to be distraction free while dealing with whatever Zeke had for us.

I quickly washed and dressed in the only clean shirt and jeans I had left by the time my computer was up and running. I logged in, then grabbed a beer before settling back down at the table. It didn't take long before Zeke's face popped up on my screen.

"What's going on?" I asked, taking a gulp.

"We got confirmation of a transport shipment in the middle of the gulf tonight. Sketch is on his way down to New Orleans with Trey and Toren. We need you to get down there to back them up."

"Where's the fed on this?" I knew where the fed was. Hiding behind our fucking skirts as per fucking usual. I scowled. I was over this bullshit, cleaning up their fucking messes.

"That's the kicker. The owner of the ship is an American-born Hungarian Oligarch. There are a lot of political sensitivities and they're not touching this. So basically, they want us to do their dirty work, so it doesn't look like a federal hit."

"Of course," I replied dryly. "What's the timeline?"

"I got a private flight for you out of Staunton in about two hours. Get your shit done and on the plane. Sketch will meet you in New Orleans."

"We have any contacts out there?" I started gathering my things, leaving my chat still going.

"Potentially. I'm trying to reach out to them now. I should have something on the books for you when you get into the city." I could hear Zeke's fingers flying over the keyboard. "Drive fast. It will take you two hours to get to Staunton."

"Sounds like a challenge to me." I threw the dirty clothes into a bag and gathered my guns and equipment into their cases. "Do I have clearance for my weapons?" While I could check my guns, I don't want to leave them to chance for them to be tampered with or stolen.

"Weapons are clear. It's one of ours that's flying."

"Roger. Logging off now. I'll catch you later." I logged off the computer and slid my laptop into its special protective case. I tossed a twenty-dollar bill on the table for housekeeping, then grabbed my bags and headed to the truck.

The glint of sunlight off chrome had me glancing towards the back of the building. I recognized the bike. My stomach sank at the potential implication. The bike started with a loud, grumbling roar. I gave a slight nod at the man on the machine and took off down the road.

Fifteen minutes later, I pulled off onto a side road and into a vacant parking lot. The road was obscured by a tree line, so we were relatively safe. I got out of the cab, just as the bike pulled in behind me. Dressed in head-to-toe black leather, the six-foot-nine behemoth of a man sauntered over to me.

"What's going on, Dawson?" With his long black hair pulled back into a ponytail and his aviator glasses, Dawson fitted the dangerous biker profile to a T. Dawson was a well-known entity among the underground as a mercenary. He was a neutral party, and didn't belong to any known group or organization, which for him made him a high commodity. He knew where all the bodies were buried, or oftentimes, where the ashes went. He got along great with Sketch when we first met in Congo. We were on a rescue mission, looking for some high-profile diplomats that had been taken by a terrorist organization. Dawson was on a kill order. Our paths crossed when we were on an op, and we didn't kill each other. Our association was completely secret and only used when absolutely necessary. It didn't bode well if he was here for me. "You've been marked, Parker," Dawson said, grimly.

My stomach dropped. "Evie." Her name escaped my lips on a panicked breath.

"I was called up for you, not for her."

It should have been a bit of relief, but it wasn't. Dawson being called up was a pretty big deal. He only took on the highest profile of calls. "Who placed the order?" My fists were clenched. I knew the answer but I needed him to confirm it.

"Order came through the Council, at the request of the Cruz Cartel."

"When and what's the order?" My back went ramrod straight, and my jaw clenched.

"The order was placed three weeks ago, for capture and/or kill with explicit delivery orders. I was sent to Nashville to look for you, but I had just missed you," He replied with a smirk. My chest heaved at the implication. Nothing mission sensitive happened in Nashville, except for ...

"They saw me with Evie?" I questioned softly. It was the only explanation I could think of.. She was followed to Nashville.

"They saw you getting cozy with the girl. That didn't sit right with The Banker or Sebastian Cruz. I'll figure out something to throw them off track, but in the meantime, stay the fuck away from the girl."

"Yeah, that's not going to happen. What's the delivery date?" This would really fuck up my plans if it was soon.

"There isn't one. I made up an excuse that I had other priorities, and they were surprisingly fine with it. They said this was a low priority, so I figured they're only pissed that you got close for the one night." Dawson replied, as he pulled out his pack of cigarettes and lit one.

"I owe you," I said simply.

Dawson snorted. "Brother, the debt will never come due. Think of it as thank you for the gifts you left me," he replied with an evil grin. Dawson's wife was taken hostage by one of the tribes during a humanitarian mission. We were there to rescue her, and because he was on a mission, Dawson didn't even know she had been taken. We were able to get her to safety, and came back to help Dawson take care of business.

"What do you need me to do?" I asked wearily. I felt torn, the need to be with Evie warred against the common sense option of going to New Orleans with Sketch and the rest of the team.

"Do what you're planning to do. I wanted to give you a head's up that eyes are on you. You know the drill. I may have taken the order, but it's possible they also farmed this out to someone outside of the Syndicate." Dawson warned. He wasn't the only mercenary for hire, but he was the best and he got shit done.

"Keep your coms on you, we may be meeting up sooner than you think," I said, slapping his hand and pulling him into a half hug.

"Roger."

I climbed back into the truck and watched Dawson ride away. He could have easily taken me out. While we worked together one time, he truly didn't need to reach out to me. Allies like that were hard as hell to come by and I was grateful for him.

I put my foot on the gas and sped toward Staunton airport. Thankfully, I got there with ten minutes to spare. I handed my bags to the female attendant and boarded the plane in a huff. Normally these flights are shared charters, meaning a bunch of rich folks are traveling to the same destination, and they have empty seats. I kept my sunglasses on and tugged on the blazer jacket that I always brought with me. You never knew who you'll have to impress or schmooze. Noah called me the play-boy, as I could charm the panties, or pants, off anyone. My track record seemed to agree with it.

Thankfully, I was the sole person on the plane and which I was grateful. The attendant was very attentive, and while I knew she was offering something more, I declined. I still had the taste of Evie on my lips and it wasn't something I would easily give up.

We touched down at a private airfield outside of the city. I stepped out of the plane. The Louisiana humidity hit me like a ton of bricks. The dark clouds threatened a storm, and I could only see that as an omen.

"About fucking time you got here." The deep voice of my buddy, Toren, rumbled to my right. The bald-headed beast of a man was dressed similar to me in a blazer, jeans and a button-down shirt.

"Yeah, well. Shit takes longer when you're told at the last minute you need to go wheels up," I shot back. I hustled down the stairs and slapped his open palm. I shrugged off my blazer and winced at the sweat already building under my shirt.

"We can compare sit reps when we get to base. What did you bring?" Toren replied. I handed him my carry-on bag and grabbed my duffle and the case carrying my equipment.

"A couple of Glocks, an AR-47, and some grenades." My response was nonchalant, but it showed how dangerous and serious the situation was.

"It fits." Toren nodded as we headed to his blacked-out SUV sitting a few feet away on the tarmac. We threw our bags into the back and got into the SUV.

"Is there a place to crash out or do laundry? I don't care but you guys might."

"You're a fucking child, you know that? Why didn't you do it at your girl's house?" Toren smirked, as he started the engine. My eyebrow arched in question and a growl escaped my lips before I even realized it. Zeke gossiped like a fucking schoolgirl, so it was only a matter of time before everyone knew about Evie. While I expected some shit-stirring, there was no way I was going to let it slide. Protectiveness ran through me.

"Yeah, we're not going to do that. Don't start shit about my girl," I warned.

Toren's hands held up in mock surrender. "I wouldn't dream of it. I'm just asking."

"Yeah, well don't ask," I grumped. "So give me the rundown. What's the latest?"

"Same report Zeke gave you earlier. There's a small yacht out in the middle of the Gulf, belonging to an American-born Hungarian Oligarch, with some sensitive US political ties. By our best count, there are about twelve souls on the ship."

"And to state the obvious, are we sure that they're being trafficked and it's not some rich dude's porn dream?" I drawled, as I leaned my head against the window. The lack of sleep was catching up to me and the urge to close my eyes was hefty.

"Not that there's much of a difference, but I'm pretty sure that we can differentiate between consenting partygoers and trafficking victims, you fuck. I'm pretty sure the women in zip ties being shoved into the galley means they're not there for a party," Toren growled at me.

I waved my hand away. "Sometimes you have to ask to be sure. So we have to bust our asses, get these women to safety, and then what? It magically goes away?"

"Yep. Basically." Toren shrugged. Getting dicked over by the feds wasn't anything new, particularly when they didn't want to get their hands caught in the cookie jar.

"I mean hell, it's not like it's the first time a cabinet-level secretary has been called out for trafficking women," I said with a snort. "Let me reach out to Travis and see if I can't get anything new."

I sent a quick text to my information dealer. While Zeke had his eyes and ears in pretty much every dark web spot, it was always good to collaborate your information from different sources

Any info about an upcoming show with an American-born oligarch who currently has a boat right now in the Gulf?

While we waited, I spit-balled potential names who could be part of this yacht party. I went through the mental rolodex of underworld fuckers that we haven't heard from in a while, but we couldn't agree on a theory.

Fifteen minutes later, I got my response.

"It depends on the price." This jerk. I swear ever since he won against me in a poker tournament down in Raleigh, the man thinks he's god's gift.

"Man—go fuck yourself. Do you have any info or not?"

"Potentially. Senator Gerald Jasper's name is being tossed around the dark web in conjunction with a porn cruise that's out in the Gulf of Mexico. The names of the organizers and owners aren't being revealed. But it could be the same boat.

Good to know. Any other names? I text back.

A few minutes later.

What do you know of Thomas Greenhall?

"Thomas Greenhall? Another name for Tommy Green?" I wondered aloud.

Toren scoffed. "Possible. I haven't heard that name before, but it could be someone else within that whole damn family. Lord knows they multiply like rabbits.

"Possibly. What's the story?" I texted back.

"His name has been connected to Senator Jasper. Apparently there's been some.. discussion among the rank and file members about the influence Greenhall is having, particularly with Senator Jasper.

I looked over at Toren. "Could it be Elias? We haven't heard about him in a hot minute."

Toren snorted, his dark eyes cutting over to me and giving me that bullshit look. "There's not any way that's Elias."

"I mean—hell it could be."

"Nah, it really can't."

I threw my hands up in a huff. "I'm not fucking Steve, so you're going to need to give me a clue."

Toren's eyebrows went up into his forehead. "Did you just compare me to Steve from Blue's Clues?"

"Yeah, you're his much older grandpa. I don't know. Fucking focus. Why the hell can't it be Elias?

He smirked. "Because he caught the pointy end of my katana when you were playing around with Jonesy. Sketch met me over in Arkansas, there was an old-fashioned shootout. But then I got bored, so I introduced him to my blade."

If Sketch had me worried about his humanity, Toren would have made me worried for everyone else's. Whereas Sketch was a psychopath with a heart, Toren was completely different. His victims weren't blameless but they weren't the monsters Sketch and I preferred to hunt. Toren had no boundaries, no morals and sure as hell no conscience.

I shook my head at his words and texted a thank you to Travis, making plans to visit his brother's distillery down in North Carolina before shoving my phone into my bag.

"How much longer?" I mumbled with my eyes closed and my head against the rest.

"Two fucking minutes, princess. There's coffee in the office." There went any chance for a cat nap. I opened my eyes as we pulled into the industrial marina. Fishing boats and large container ships filled the piers, and it was only a matter of time before we pulled up to a small outbuilding next to a large fishing boat. We silently got out, grabbed my gear, and hauled it into the small shack of an outbuilding. It was no bigger than my kitchen, with a sink, an old coffee pot with potentially hazardous liquid brewing, and a bathroom that barely fit a sink and toilet. The air smelled fishy, and I tried not to gag at the sight of loose shrimp shells on the bow.

"Well, Sketch. These are lovely accommodations," I quipped. My temperament was falling short due to the lack of sleep. But I wasn't happy to be away from Evie. Not again.

"Yeah, well, it was the best we could do with the time we had," Sketch snipped back. He threw a granola bar at me. "We'll grab grub on the way home. I want you to fit into the wetsuit and not have to crap your pants while you're holding a gun to some douche on a yacht."

I rolled my eyes and inhaled the bar.

"Let's figure out what we're doing so we can get it done and go back home," I muttered.

Toren laid out blown-up images of the yacht onto the cracked teal linoleum table. "We did some preliminary casing while you were playing house in bum-fuck Virginia. The ship hasn't ventured into US waters, and the US Coast Guard was also told to stand down in the event of any activity. By projections, its course is taking them in this direction. We're going to cut them off."

"What's stopping them from checking it out?" I wondered, as I moved through the pictures. The Red Lady was an odd name for a yacht, but whatever.

"Sims," Sketch replied, looking closely at the boat. The name of Kate's former FBI partner gave me a bit of relief. Even after all the crap the bureau put her through, he stuck by us and helped us out on occasion when he could.

"The plan is to take control of the ship and bring it back here. Sims will be here waiting, with EMS and social services on standby," Toren stated.

"By any means necessary?" I asked. I glanced over at the weaponry we had. With only the three of us, we would need some serious firepower. Sketch was our weapons guru and kept track of all of his shiny toys.

"Well duh. Do you think we're going to go in and ask politely?" Sketch smirked. "Current surveillance by drone suggests here are only three men on board. Heat signatures confirm multiple smaller stature or women are below deck," Trey mentioned, as he loaded his rifle.

"How many are we talking about?" I asked.

"At least twenty," Toren replied grimly. Fuck. That was too many for only the four of us.

Sketch threw me a wetsuit. "I want to get out on to the water before the sun goes down. Let's roll out."

We grabbed our gear and weapons and made our way to the boat. The old shrimp boat had definitely seen better days, and I was surprised as hell when it rumbled to a start with ease. After pulling out of the harbor, we cruised at mid-throttle for about an hour, until we slowed down to a crawl. With nothing around us, we dropped the anchor, along with fishing lines.

Our boat went dark as we waited for the other boat to come into view. It took about three hours, but finally our drone sighted the ship, about two clicks out.

While Toren dropped the dingy and Sketch sorted the closed-circuit SCUBA tanks, I went to the head, took a leak, then shucked off my clothes. I pulled up the wetsuit with a grimace. I hated feeling like a damn sausage in these damn things. With everything loaded up in the dinghy and Trey maintaining the boat, we took off. Toren at the engine, we quietly made our way closer to the ship. Toren stopped the engine a quarter mile away. Sketch counted down with his hands and fell backward into the deep blue waters. I followed right behind him.

After thirty minutes of swimming, we reached the boat. It was a sixty foot yacht, small by billionaire standards, but low enough profile to not be conspicuous.

"No movement." Toren's voice said through our ears. We took this as a sign to keep going and crept up the ladder. Stilled silence met us as we landed on the deck, our rifles at the ready. My hair prickled at the back of my neck. Something didn't feel right. I looked over at Sketch with a raised eyebrow. His eyes narrowed as he looked around. He motioned forward, and I veered to the left. Our senses on alert, we made our way around the exterior, searching for any movement or noise. Nothing.

Something was really off.

We met up at the stairs and while he covered my back, I went down first. The door slid to an open galley. No souls were around. We went through the whole area and didn't find a single soul. The ship's autopilot was engaged with a course marked for Havana.

My eyes caught Sketch's.

"We've been fucking duped," Sketch muttered through his mask.

"Engine bay?" I wondered. I made my way forward to the hull of the ship, looking for a trap door of some kind. It took a while, but I found pulley door, underneath the carpet next to the lavatory. After a couple of pulls, it finally popped open. The smell of human waste and vomit wafted up the stairs and my stomach dropped.

I flicked on my flashlight and winced in horror. Women and young teenage boys and girls, all tied up and gagged, sat on the floor. Three babies with tear-stained cheeks laid in a box. They looked up at me vacantly with glassy eyes. Fury and rage battled for dominance against despair for these lives.

"Found them," I called up to Sketch. "Radio it in. Tell them we have women, minors, and infants." I walked over to one of the women, a blonde with a swollen pregnant belly, who was the closest. I pulled the gag off her, and she looked at me tearfully.

"Do you speak English?" She looked at me with worry in her eyes and nodded.

"Thank god. We'll get you back to shore ASAP. Who was with you? Where did they go?"

"I don't know where they went. There were three of them. A woman. Her name was Hadley someone. Two men. One was called Mack and the other was Thomas. We've been on this boat forever. The babies. They were crying for so long. I don't think they can cry anymore," her broken English whispered.

"Can you please help untie them? We're going to bring this boat to the States and we'll have people ready to take care of you." I gently picked up one of the infants, the smell radiating from the small thing was horrific.

"There are no supplies. We've been here for a couple of days now. No formula. No diapers. Nothing."

"Echo, search for some cloths, dish towels, something. These babies are in bad shape." I called up the stairs.

"Delta, you need to come up and see this."

Fuck. This didn't sound good. I handed the baby back to the woman. "Can you please help me untie everyone?" She nodded and took the baby out of my hands.

I climbed back up the ladder and joined Sketch at the helm. He was looking out with his binoculars, his jaw tight.

"We got four adults, a bunch of teenagers, and three infants all needing medical assistance. What's going on?" He wordlessly handed me the binoculars. A ship was approaching fast. Fear brought my heart into my throat.

"We got time to get out of here?"

"Trey is on his way to provide back-up. Toren is offline—must be having a coms issue. I've been trying to disengage the autopilot but it's not working. Zeke is on the line, trying to do it remotely but nothing is fucking working." He grabbed his gun. "Look for weapons. And keep the hostages down there." The boat was still moving but we couldn't deviate from the current course.

I shouted instructions for them to stay silent and in the hull while we took care of business. The approaching boat slowed to a crawl, gliding up next to us. A lone figure came out of the captain's nest.

"We're not entertaining guests," Sketch shouted over to the driver.

The figure's hands were held up over his head. "I am only here to talk," they called back.

"Then talk, fucker." I yelled back.

"I have information you may want."

The sound of a fist hitting skin was heard. "I'm here," Toren's voice came on the line.

"About fucking time," I muttered. My weapons were still trained on the shadows of the boat.

A rustling noise and sounds of another scuffle ensued before Toren came back on the line. "Bringing him aboard. You're going to want to talk with him."

"Fine. Climb up," I barked. We were taking a risk. A huge risk. With only two of us on board who could shoot, who the hell knew what this fool was packing once he made it on board. With Toren having our back and Trey coming, I felt better about sitting out here.

We watched as the figure climbed up the ladder. With our guns trained to his head as it popped over the side, my jaw dropped.

"Maks Alexeyevs." Evie's dead husband was apparently not so dead.

THIRTEEN

Evie

WIFE? Are you fucking kidding me? My internal rage remained hidden. I kept my face blank and my emotions in check. Any sort of reaction, emotional or physical, would have caused an even bigger reaction from Sebastian. The smile he gave me curdled my stomach, as he wrapped his arm around my waist.

"With the merger of our families, the power our adversaries will come against will be insurmountable. Our enemies will fall to their knees or face the consequences. The Syndicate will be stronger. Our competition is now weak and will crumble at our feet."

Lukewarm cheers came from the audience. I could see the weariness in their faces. Power was king, and with this merger, Sebastian and the Cruz Cartel stood to rule the kingdom. That fact was not lost to the leaders of the other crime organizations.

"Soon the world will come to recognize this new world

order. Governments and kingdoms will either fall in line or die on the battlefield. We will continue to ascend to greatness!" Sebastian paused and looked around. "The Cruz Cartel is only one of many organizations who make up this vast network of allies, and we look forward to a very prosperous future. All in blood, all for the Syndicate!"

"All in blood, all for the Syndicate!" repeated the crowd.

"However." He held up his hands and everyone quieted down. "We are only as strong as our weakest link. We have to have faith and truth within our Syndicate, or we will fall to our own demise. Information has been reaching people it shouldn't. Product is going missing. Our customers are becoming less trusting of our security and are scaling back their purchases. We have a fucking mole in our midst." Sebastian glared around the room. "I shouldn't have to tell you all how to lead your organizations. But trust me when I say this. I will find out who is running their damn mouth. And when I do, their leadership will also pay the price. That entire group will burn. So get your fucking houses in order."."

With a pregnant pause, Sebastian continued. "The auction is about to take place. Take this time, enjoy the products of our labor. We'll reconvene tomorrow." He gestured to the cage above him.

And with that, Sebastian pulled me off the dais and into the shadows of the tunnels. The sounds of the cage being lowered and hitting the ground with a thud sent shivers down my spine.

"I'm under no illusion you're happy about this situation. But I hope you kept your wedding dress." His cruel smile sent terror through my veins, but I kept my face placid.

"I donated it after my wedding," I replied simply.

"It doesn't matter. In a week's time, it'll be done. Evie, I intend for this to be a real marriage. Your dead husband didn't get his heir, but I will. So, forget about those visits to

Nashville or Vegas. Your only purpose is to incubate my child."

My stomach turned to lead. Maks didn't get his heir, but not for his lack of trying. I never wanted children, and I particularly didn't want to raise a child in this life. When I turned eighteen, I went to visit my abuela in Mexico, and had my fallopian tubes removed. Two months before the fateful day I met Cole. If Sebastian knew I was unable to have children, I would be as dead as his enemies.

Sebastian didn't wait for my answer and left me alone in the hallway. I took my dismissal and hurried back down the tunnel, praying the nausea and bile to stay at bay. I hoped the listening device that I dropped in the corner took in everything what was just said.

I made it to the bar before I hurtled myself into the bathroom and fell to my knees in front of the toilet, retching again, only to have nothing come out. I refused to be part of this any longer. There was nothing more I could do at this point. If I didn't leave now, this would be my death.

I rinsed out my mouth and made my way back into the office. I logged onto my social media account, and posted in the book suggestion group where I knew Zeke and his team would be watching.

Looking for a romantasy with a heroic but quiet Afro-Mexican FMC who loves a dark and morally gray Black nerd that wears glasses.

I knew it was corny, but it was something agreed upon by Zeke and I. It triggered my escape plan and it started the countdown. I had two hours before I would meet with someone who would help transfer me to a safehouse. I needed to get home, to get everything together. There was already a go-bag sitting in the back of my closet with a couple of changes of clothes, cash, and a gun. But it would take forever to get Mario into his damn crate. I considered dropping him off with Angela and Chris so I could just leave. I sent all the encrypted documents, ledgers, and other information into my encrypted cloud server, specifically created for Zeke and his team. I was ready to execute the plan. But I didn't take into account my primary mode of transportation would be destroyed.

This town was too small for an Uber or taxi service. And while I could walk, it would look really weird if I did. I needed to steal someone's car or borrow one.

I gathered up the laptop, bank receipts and cash bag, and shoved them into my bag, then hooked it over my shoulder. I wandered down the hall, taking my time, when I got to the bar. Even though everything inside of me screamed for me to run away quickly.

"Hey, Roger, I'm feeling like shit. Can I borrow your car?" My shoulders slumped and I let my eyes droop. I wasn't lying. My body was still sore from the night before and probably exacerbated by the anxiety and stress flowing through my veins. The old man looked at me with his bushy white eyebrows raised.

He tossed me the keys and nodded to the back door. I lifted my chin in thanks. "I'll bring it back tomorrow," I lied. I had no intention of bringing him back his car. I planned to leave it at the park-n-ride, where I planned on meeting up with a Rainbow Trail volunteer, who would get me to my meeting location with Zeke's team.

I climbed into his late model silver sedan and took off for my house. Because it was the middle of the afternoon, it took longer than I anticipated driving the seven miles. By the time I managed to pull into my driveway, my nerves were shot. I hurried inside and tossed my bags onto the couch, and ran for my bedroom as quickly as my aching body could. I went into the hall closet and grabbed the black bookbag and hustled into the kitchen. I threw my wallet, burner phone, laptops, cash bag, and back-up USBs into the bag, along with the bag of toiletries I kept on hand. I forwent trying to corral the boss, so I scooped out food into a large container for Mario, and sent Angela and Chris instructions, telling them I needed to fly back to Mexico to visit my grandmother. A pang of fear shot through me. I had weaknesses, and if there was anything I feared most, it was they would be collateral damage. I sent my Uncle Miguel a text and asked him to bring Abuelita to his house on the other side of the country. Miguel was familiar with what my father was involved in and never agreed to joining the life. He was my father's brother and refused to take part in this life which had corrupted so many.

I grabbed the king of the house and kissed his black and white head. "You be good for Chris and Angela, okay? I love you so much." I knew they would take great care of him. This wasn't going to be permanent and after everything calmed down, I planned to scoop my baby back up.

I grabbed a hammer and my phone out to the garage. This was the last step before I left. Just as I was about to take a hammer to it, it rang. An unknown number comes across the screen. I hesitated and debated. The ringing stopped, then started again. A feeling of dread came over me.

"Hello?" I answered cautiously.

"Where did you go, Evelyn? Imagine me coming to look for my bride to be, to get to know her, and then to be surprised when she's not waiting for me in her office." Sebastian's voice portrayed a calmness I didn't believe.

"I'm still feeling the effects from yesterday. I was planning to rest for the rest of the day," I replied quietly.

"Do you think I'm stupid?"

"Excuse me?" I stammered.

"Do you honestly think I'm dumb? Do you think I believe

anything you say? When I said that this would be a real marriage, I meant what I said, Evelyn. You're going to be in my bed, chained, if need be, until you're pregnant and I have my heir."

"I don't understand." My heart raced and I tried to move back into the house without making a sound. Or breathe. Silence filled my ears. I double checked my screen to make sure he didn't actually hang up, and I was about to speak when suddenly he did.

"I see everything, Evelyn." With that ominous statement, the phone hung up.

Fuckity Fuck fuck fuck. I dropped my phone onto the counter with a clatter and grabbed my bookbag. Then I ran back through the house, and made sure everything was locked up, before running out to Roger's car.

I stuttered to a stop when I saw a large, black SUV sitting behind his car.

"No," I groaned.

Jimmy got out of the driver's seat. "Mr. Cruz would like to see you back at the bar."

I shook my head slowly. "Jimmy, please. I don't feel well. I need to get to the doctor."

A conflicted look crossed his eyes. "Just following orders, Ma."

My stomach dropped, and fear raged through my veins. This is it.

"Jimmy. Please. You know this isn't right. Neither one of us should be wrapped up in this. Please," I whimpered.

"Get in the car, Evelyn." The brusque tone of his voice surprised me. I gauged the distance between us to see if I could make it.

Suddenly, strong arms wrapped across my torso, and I

struggled. I fought against the hold. I used my legs, kicking at anything and everything I could.

"Jimmy, please! Please let me go!" I begged.

"It'll be all right, Ma. I promise." The strong arms lifted me, half carried me, half dragged me to the SUV.

A sweet smelling cloth went over my mouth and nose, and I struggled harder, fighting with everything I had.

"No! Please!" I slurred.

I tumbled into something hard.

A car door slammed.

Lights out.

FOURTEEN

Cole

"I DIDN'T HAVE ghost hunting on the bucket list, but here we are," I muttered, my arms out in position to shoot. Sketch grunted in agreement, but his gaze didn't waive from his scope on Maks.

"Zeke has eyes on the sky right now. He tapped into the closest imagery satellite, and I have the drones," Trey's voice muttered through my ear. Sketch sent me a side glance and I nodded.

Toren popped up right behind Maks and kept his gun against Maks's head.

"You're here for a reason and I don't have time for bullshit. Mind telling us what's going on?" I called out. Maks raised one hand over his head and lifted his shirt with the other, showing us a lean body covered in tattoos, but clean of weapons. Regardless, we didn't relent and kept our guns locked on his face. The moment Sketch got the feeling, he would be likely to shoot.

"I'm obviously very much alive. I have your government to thank," Maks said with a smug smile.

"Start fucking talking, or I'm going to get pissed off," Sketch growled, his finger tightening on the trigger. "Who owns this ship and where was this cargo going to?"

Maks shrugged and gave a slick grin. "Hadley Almasi. She is the wife of the Hungarian diplomat, Ferenc Almasi. The two countries are in the middle of a treaty negotiation. My job is to ensure delivery to the right buyer before this treaty is signed."

The contents of my stomach curdled. The feds were aware of what was on this ship, which meant they were involved.

"What kind of fuckery are you talking about? So you're just what? A delivery boy? You're running these women and kids to a potential buyer, so they can save face with their treaties?" I snapped. I knew there was corruption within our government, but fuck. I couldn't imagine how far up this went.

"When it comes to the government, is any deal truly cut and dry? No, of course not. Your team, of all people, should know the fuckery that takes place behind the scenes. Your government is turning a blind eye to Ms. Hadley's dealings, because the price of a couple women and children are not worth the price of global diplomacy and domination. Hungary is granting the US access to mineral rights, military air space, and above all, their allyship."

"In exchange for?" Toren demanded.

"Removal of sanctions, military weapons and some other political bullshit I don't care about." Maks waved his hand around like the details were too inconsequential to remember.

"Who is she working with?" Sketch grunted out.

Maks smile turned sinister. "Thomas Greenhall. But I'm

sure you know him better as Thomas Cruz. Tommy Green? The man has so many names. Either way. He's hell bent on taking over the Syndicate and doing everything he can to undermine Sebastain. So he's going after his trade and products first. He's making inroads now, with various suppliers. And he's already infiltrated Sebastian's closest circle"

Thomas Cruz, otherwise known as Tommy Green, was like the cockroach that never went away.

"Don't call the scum who steal women and children fucking 'suppliers'," Sketch snarled. He lowered his weapon and stalked over to Maks. "If you're working for Thomas Green, and you're working for the feds, you're double crossing everyone. I don't trust a single word you're saying. Where does your loyalty actually lie?"

"Myself. I don't care who takes over the Syndicate. I don't care if it all comes crashing down. Sebastain Cruz destroyed the Alexyandez Bratva. My Bratva. A once thriving legacy has been demolished because of his need to overcompensate for his lack of brains and dick. I want to fucking ruin him. If I can get Thomas Cruz to take out Sebastian, then all the feds have to do is take down Tommy."

Sketch looked at me and shrugged. The idea had some validity. Killing one serpent is better than killing two. And who the hell knows, maybe they'd kill each other in the process.

"Then what the fuck are you doing with the feds?" I growled.

Maks shrugged. "Insurance. If Thomas fails, the feds step in. Either way, I am a free man."

Toren snorted. "You've got to be fucking kidding me. What happens if Thomas doesn't kill Sebastain? Or they decide to work together?"

Maks's smug grin faltered. "Uh huh. I guess you didn't think of that." I sneered. "Use your fucking brain Maks. Once you have outlived your usefulness, you're going to be trashed like the others. You're not the only person he has in his little bag of tricks." I smirked, watching as he deflated.

"I am not stupid," he spat out. He crossed his arms over his chest. "There are a lot of players involved than originally thought. It would be best if your team leaves them alone."

Toren scoffed. "Yeah, like we'll believe you." He nudged the tip of his rifle to Maks head. "Get your ass inside the cabin. We're not going to do this while we're sitting out in the open."

Suddenly, all the power in the boat shut down, leaving us in a blanket of darkness. The tell-tale thump thump thump sound indicated a helicopter was approaching.

"Trey, we've got more incoming!" I pressed the button to my ear piece. Silence greeted me. "Zeke?" Static filled my ears. I unhooked my ear piece in frustration. "Fuck! Comms are down!"

"Get inside now!" A red laser dot suddenly appeared on Toren's forehead.

"Get down!" Toren grabbed Maks by the collar and dragged him down, just as a thunderous shot ran through the air.

"Don't anyone move!" the voice above us thundered. The chopper was right over us. A rope dropped down in front of us, attached from the bird above. "Drop your weapons now. On the ground. Now! I have targets on all of you fuckers. You do not want to test me."

I glanced at my crew and nodded. Laser markers landed on all of our chests. We had to hope Trey and Zeke realized something was up. Because right now, we were screwed. We laid down the rifles we had in our hands but kept the knives and other weapons hidden on our persons.

A body swung down the ropes and dropped to his feet

before us. He was about as tall as I was, but leaner. His pointed nose and green eyes were as familiar as Sebastian's.

"Tommy Cruz," I drawled. My fingers itched to pull the fucking trigger of the gun I had hidden in my waistband, and I could tell by Sketch's rigid stature that he wanted to do the same. The red laser still focused on Toren's chest, so we didn't move a muscle.

"Gentleman. I understand this isn't the ideal scenario. But I needed your attention. If you behave, we'll let you leave in one piece." Tommy unhooked the rope from his belt and sauntered over to us.

Sketch scoffed. "You could have called."

"Yeah, a letter would have been nice. We haven't seen you in so long, Tommy," I crooned sarcastically. We hadn't seen this man in over five months. "We keep missing you."

Tommy smirked. What I wouldn't give to wipe the arrogant smirk off this fucker's face with the blunt end of my knife. I grinned back, as ideas on how to end this fucker swirled in my head. Tommy threw a cellphone to Sketch, who caught it. "Text your fearless leader. We need to have a meeting."

Sketch growled. "First of all, we're not at your beck and call. If you want a meeting, set it up with our admin."

My head swiveled over at Sketch. "Since when do we have an admin?"

"Seriously? Do you not pay attention to your emails? We sent out an announcement last week," Sketch muttered angrily, his attention kept on Tommy.

"You know I don't read my work emails. I wait until I get into the office and I'm surprised," I replied back. My hands drifted to the straps of my waterproof tactical bag laid on my chest, where my knife was concealed inside the nylon. As Tommy was distracted watching Sketch's meltdown, I slowly inched the handle down.

Sketch groaned and rubbed his eyes. "I can't believe this. This is why you haven't turned in your annual review yet?"

I shrugged. "I was waiting for Kate to get back to show me how to use the new program."

A shot rang out and Maks crumbled, his screams piercing the night. "You are wasting my fucking time." Tommy snapped. Maks's cries quieted as blood pooled around his knee. "He won't die yet but your brutish friend over there will if you don't shut the fuck up and dial in your captain."

Sketch, glared at Tommy and dialed in Noah's number. "Who the fuck is this?" Noah's snarl came through the speaker.

"Yo man. Tommy Cruz wants a meeting." Sketch held out the phone. "Your turn Little Cruz. Tell the big man what you want."

"Listen to me you fucking psychopath. If you want to see your Angel again, and that hell-spawn you have growing inside her, you fucking shut the hell up and let the adults talk," Tommy snapped. He turned to me. "I have eyes on all your weaknesses, so you need to hear what I have to say".

Oh shit. Tommy just fucked up by threatening my sister. I was all for the beast to be released now. I was really wanting to play with my toys, but now? Ah hell no, this fucker was done.

My back straightened and my gaze narrowed.

"Go on." Noah's voice came through the speaker. I knew he had Zeke with him at our shop, and they were tracing this call.

"We have a common enemy. One who needs to be eradicated immediately."

"And your point?" I stepped forward and watched as the red dot on my chest followed my move.

Tommy cocked his head. "I propose a temporary partnership."

Toren snorted. "Why the fuck would we want to partner with you? You're the fucking enemy here."

Tommy sighed. "Despite what you may think or hear, I am not a horrible man. The Cruz Cartel, along with the Syndicate, needs new leadership. The old guard is too set in their ways and they can't get their thumbs out of their asses to see what lies ahead. I need you to take them out."

"So you want us to...what? Take out the leadership of the Syndicate so you can come into power?" I questioned. "Why would we help one snake take out the other?"

"Because hunting one snake is better than hunting two." Tommy's eyebrows arched. "And because you have no choice."

Sketch's eyes narrowed at Tommy, the only reaction on his face. "And why don't we have a choice?"

An alert came from Tommy's watch. "Noah, please tell them what you just received."

Noah cleared his throat, then his voice came through. "It's a video of two women tied up." My blood ran cold and my face fell blank.

"Name the women, Noah," Tommy called out. His eyes held my glare as a knowing smile came across his face.

"Lucy and... Evie." A snarl left my lips at the same time a feral growl came from Toren. He vibrated with anger as he took a step forward. But he was too late. Within a blink, I had Tommy up against the rail, with my knife to his throat.

"What the fuck did you do?" I thundered. Tommy's body remained calm, but rigid.

"I didn't take them," he managed.

"Where are they? Where is my wife?" I roared. I bent him back over the railing, the blade of my lightly digging into his skin. Enough to draw blood, but not enough to kill him. Yet.

Sketch pulled me off him. "Let him talk. Then you can kill him," he muttered in my ear.

I shook him off and pointed the knife back at Tommy. "Fucking talk before I yank out your damn tongue."

"Sebastian has been tracking Evie. He figured out her scheme a while ago. That's why the deliveries have all been fucked up and no one has been able to stop any transport. She's safe. For now. But don't worry, he has plans for her."

My body shook in rage as fire raced through my veins. Sketch stepped in front of me and managed to get me to catch his eye. "We will take care of her. We will get her back."

I nodded. If there was anyone who could help get me back, it was Sketch.

I glared at Tommy. "You didn't answer the fucking question. Where is my wife?" I thundered.

"That's not how this works. I'm not giving up my only leverage.. Agree to help me take down Sebastian, then I'll send you her location. If you don't agree, fine. We don't care if they're collateral damage when we go after them ourselves."

"Fine. We're in." I snapped. Sketch jerks his head in my direction but I ignored his warning glare.

"I figured you'd understand. Like I said. I didn't have anything to do with this. I have some of my own embedded within his faction. Trafficking women and children isn't my preferred method of bringing in money," Tommy replied with a wink.

"We take down Sebastian, which we were planning to do anyway. What's our benefit to this grand scheme of yours? What's to say we don't go out and find these women ourselves?" Sketch asked. His hands clenched in fists.

"Or take you down with him?" I shot

Tommy grinned, his face turning maniacal. "You don't have the manpower to take me down. There's what? Fifteen, twenty of you? Tops? You would be out of your fucking element. Your team would be dead within minutes. You couldn't be able to go against the Syndicate without decimating your team. You get your women back. I gain control. I'll even throw in this bonus. If you take out every single governing body on the Syndicate council, I'll stop the Syndicate's position in the skin trade."

Sketch crossed his arms in disbelief, his eyebrow arching. "Yeah right. You're going to take away their biggest source of income and they're going to be fine with that? You're fucking delusional," he scoffed.

Toren snorted. "How the fuck do we know we can trust you?"

Tommy shrugged. "You really can't. But as a peace offering and to show you how invested I am, they're no longer in Virginia. They moved the girls down here to Louisiana, outside of New Orleans. Near Pilottown." Tommy touched his watch again, then hooked the rope back to his waist. "I'll send you the coordinates and timing. Be ready within the next twenty-four hours."

"How can we be sure your team won't shoot us in the back?"

"You can't be sure. I don't give a fuck what you trust in or believe in. Just make sure the leadership of the Syndicate is dead, and you'll be fine. Otherwise, maybe don't turn around," Tommy said with a smug grin. "Just do what you normally do, boys. Blow shit up." He paused. "And you can have this punk. He'll be dead soon, anyway. He's outlived his usefulness." He pressed a button on his watch and was lifted away, like a deranged male Mary Poppins.

"FUCK!" Toren screamed.

Suddenly, the power came back on. I heard a clicking sound coming from my ear piece and plugged it back in.

"Zeke?" I called out, my voice cracking. Evie was in trouble and my heart sank. I hated feeling helpless. I needed to get my girl back.

"I was with Noah and heard every word. Cole, I need to tell you. Evie was done. She was trying to escape. She triggered her evac protocol at three-fifty. When she didn't make it to her pickup location by six, the person picking her up reached out to me." Dread filled my veins. knew Sebastian must have pushed her to her limit. I could only imagine what he did.

My mind raced and I patted my wetsuit and cursed. "I don't have my phone. Zeke, I put the tracking device under her shoulder blade. Look to see if it's active."

"On it." Zeke paused. "Yeah. It's active. I'm sending the coordinates to Trey. He's on his way to you now."

"Where was the fucker at? He should have been here by now!" Sketch shouted. He pressed a cloth to Maks's knee. "Call the fucking feds and tell them we need a damn medic. We have four women, and a bunch of minors and babies needing attention. Plus, a fucking ghost." He glared at the supposed dead man.

"Medic and feds are enroute. The vessel was reported stolen, so they have a way of explaining the victims. Trey was held up by Tommy's crew at multiple gunpoint, which is why he hasn't shown up. He's going to get there first, so get out of there quickly. Let the feds manage the rest."

"Got it."

We made quick work of gathering the women, teens and babies onto the deck for the fed's assistance, as Trey pulled up the old shrimp boat next to the stern of the yacht. We tossed our gear over to him and managed to get ourselves over before he took off in the opposite direction from where the feds were coming from. We changed in silence, anger pouring off us.

Finally dressed, I wandered to where Sketch and Trey were, at the wheel of the ship.

"You know where we're going?" I asked Trey.

Trey nodded. "Once we get back to the marina, she's about three hours west. There's a commercial port in Port Fourchon. Based on Evie's previous intel, that's their southern port of choice."

My heart swelled a little with pride. Even while kidnapped, all her hard work and sacrifice were still paying off.

Sketch looked over at me, his gray eyes critical. "You hanging in there?"

I gave a terse nod. "I'm trying to. It's taking everything in me to not go ballistic." I paused. "You know I'm not waiting for them, right? I don't care what Tommy said."

Sketch gave a grim smile. "I wouldn't expect you to. We got your back. Noah and the others are on their way out here. They left a while ago and should be at the marina by the time we get there." He smacked my shoulder. "We'll get your girl back. We just need to be smart about it."

"How's this going to work anyway?" Trey questioned, as he maintained his attention to the open waters. We were going at a fast clip, or as fast as this damn shrimp boat could go.

"Like the douchnozzle said. We do what we do best, blow shit up and kick ass, " I snapped grimly. I turned to Sketch for agreement.

"We watch our own fucking backs. Don't trust anyone on his crew. And when it's all over, well, they're all foe to me."

I nodded. "Priority number one is securing the women. If there's one fucking hair messed up on Evie's head, I'm going to make sure they don't have a scalp for their own."

Trey grunted in agreement. Without a word, Toren stalked to the bow and stayed at the rail. I watched as he gripped the rail tightly and hung his head.

I nodded at him and looked at Sketch. "Let me guess. Lucy is his girl?"

Sketch shrugged and rubbed his shaved head. "Sorta? I don't know, man. I don't keep track of everyone else's shit. But I do know Lucy was one of ours."

I looked at him with a perplexed look. "Wait. Is she the new admin?"

Sketch groaned and smacked me upside the head.

"Hey! I haven't been at the fucking center in over a couple of months. How the fuck was I supposed to know!" I snapped, rubbing my head.

"Listen, fucker. The feds had other assets at the bar. Lucy and Eugene were a grandfather-granddaughter partnership that legitimately lived in the area. They were there for observation only. They weren't to interact or interfere with anything. Lucy is the hacker Kate has worked with in the past and was in the process of poaching to Tactical Redemption, to assist Zeke on our increased efforts," Sketch said quietly, watching the waves.

"Toren met her online a few months ago and fell hard. Although he'd lie to your damn face about it," Trey mumbled. I understood. Toren had baggage. I mean, fuck, we had all baggage and trauma of some kind. But Toren came to us as someone who was barely able to function in civilized society after the death of his child by his crazy-as-fuck ex-girlfriend. It took years of therapy, medication, and a lot of good old bloody vengeance to bring him somewhat back to normal.

We spent the rest of the trip back to the marina in silence, lost in our own thoughts. Mentally preparing for the mission before us. The most important mission of my life.

"Explain it to me like I'm a kid, Cole. Because the only thing I've heard from you, aside from telling me how to run this operation, is that I broke your heart. If I broke your heart so damn badly, then I apologize." Her words went through my head. I never fully told her how much I loved her. I told her that she was mine, as if she had a choice. And while she didn't truly have a choice, I didn't want her to feel like a possession. She was born into a life without a choice. And I, like every other man in her family, took her choice away from her. Fuck. I was a dick.

She deserved so much better than what I gave her. Once I get her back, I vowed to make her understand. And I'd give her that choice. If she didn't want to be with me, I would figure out a way to live with it.

After we docked, we grabbed our gear and made our way to the parking lot. Three black SUVs waited for us, with the engines running. Noah stepped out and pulled me into a half hug. "We'll get your girl back."

I nodded, then raised my chin in greeting to the rest of the team. Along with Noah and Benji, a few of our new recruits had joined us. Zeke ambled over to us.

"Evie and Lucy are part of the family. We never leave our family behind." Zeke muttered in my ear, pulling me into him. I nodded, my heart in my throat. He released me, and I shook my head.

"Here's the fucking deal." Noah gathered us around him. "Evie and Lucy are located in Docking bay C1. By the time we get there, dawn will be breaking and we will be in between dockworker shifts. We go in, do the most fucking damage, and get those girls out. Fuck anyone else. If we can't reach the leadership, fuck Tommy and his merry band of cunts. We'll regroup and figure it out later. Those women are our priority. Check your gear, we roll up in three. Get your game faces on, fuckers." He pounded the hood of the SUV. "Let's fucking go!"

I put my AirPods into my ears and hit play on my mission playlist. "Glock in My Lap" by 21 Savage and Metro Boomin filled my ears. I climbed into the back seat and grabbed my gear bag.

I methodically started checking my gear, even though it was meticulously checked before we arrived. I mentally prepared myself and focused on the end game.

Evie would be in my arms, or I would fucking die trying.

FIFTEEN

Evie

FIFTEEN MINUTES.

That's how long I've been awake from whatever concoction Jimmy gave me. Fifteen minutes to go from barely coherent to fully conscious. Fear and panic fought for dominance, but I couldn't let it show. I needed to be calm. If I had any chance of getting out of here alive, I needed to keep my wits about me.

I looked around, at what I could barely see. It was dark, with the only light coming in from a dirty window about ten feet up. The room was more like a closet. Smaller than my office back at the bar, the bare room was nothing but concrete walls and floor. My hands were bound together, as were my ankles, with rope. My body felt like I had gone a full ten rounds in the boxing ring. A moan from the other side of the room startled me.

"What the actual fuck happened?" A familiar voice bounced off the walls. My eyes widened in shock.

"Lucy?" The crumpled form across the room groaned again. "Lucy!" I whisper shouted.

"I'm going to kill that rotten bastard," she grumbled. She managed to sit herself up. "Those fuckers took my glasses. I can't see shit."

"There's not much to see, Lucy. It's pretty dark. Are you okay?"

"Other than being tied up in a way that is not kinky, yeah. What about you? Are you good?" Her voice was raspy but sounded clear.

"I'm okay. I am so sorry you got involved with this." My gut twisted at the thought of an innocent being involved. Guilt crashed over me, and I wanted to scream.

"Girly pop, I've been involved for the last four years," she scoffed. She shook her head slightly, her purple box braids swayed with the movement. My head raised sharply at her words.

"What the hell are you talking about?" I hissed.

Before she uttered another word, the steel door to my left opened with a loud creak and a light was thrown on. Temporarily blinded, it took a minute before my eyes could see in front of me. A man I had never seen before walked in. Tall, muscular, with bronzed skin and black hair walked in.

"Well, it's about time." His southern voice boomed. He was so loud I immediately flinched. "Good to see ya up, ladies!"

"He's way too cheerful to be on our side," Lucy muttered loudly.

"Nah, com'on now. If you don't want me to be my cheerful self, I can turn back into the mean asshole I normally am." His grin grew wider, but it didn't reach his eyes. Eyes that screamed empty, almost evil.

"If you're in such a good mood, how about you let us out of here?" I asked dryly.

"That's going to be a nope." He crossed his large arms across his chest. "So, here's the plan. We're going to get both of you washed up. We have some folks coming in for the party and you guys need to be looking your best. Dirty hoes don't get the most dollars and y'all have already cost us a pretty penny. We need to make our money back." Another larger man walked in. Paler than fucking Casper, with long red hair, this fucker bigger than the first one, the one I deemed psycho in my head. Red marched over to Lucy and jerked her up by her tied hands.

Fear shot through my veins. "Hey, get the fuck away from her!" I yelled, watching as she struggled to get away. But with her hands and ankles tied together, it was futile. He dragged her out, and didn't bother looking at me or saying a word. "Evie!" She screamed.

"Lucy! I'll figure this out. I'll get you!" Panic and anger warred within me.

Psycho blond shook his head. "Honestly., I don't know why folks are causing a fuss over you. But whatever. " He walked over to me and grabbed me under my armpit. "Let's go, princess." I twisted my body and tried to kick him, but it was no use. He half carried, half walked me out into a dimly lit corridor. Steel doors lined the hall, and I desperately tried to get to a glance to see if there was anything, or anyone around that could help. The effort was in vain. As we moved through the building, I didn't see another soul. No one else was around and that worried me even more. We stopped in front of another door, where psycho banged on the frame.

The door swung open and my body tensed, ready to fight. This sonofabitch.

"Where do you want her?" the psycho asked, as if I was an inconvenient plant or object to be set aside somewhere.

"Bring her in. We're almost done with the other one,"

Jimmy's bored voice came through. My glare did nothing to dissuade him or cause any reaction. Any sort of friendly banter or relationship we had before he took me was long gone. *I'm going to kill him first.* Ways to make him hurt crossed my mind as psycho boy pulled me by my elbow and shoved me onto a cot. Fear wasn't my primary motivator any more. Fury was. I glared at both men while they had a conversation, too low for my ears. I glanced around. What looked like a hospital infirmary. Startling white walls, steel tables, and an open shower with five shower heads. No modicum of privacy. Finally, the psycho left.

"Really? After everything, this is how you fucking treat me?" I seethed. My shoulders burned from being behind my back this entire time.

Jimmy shrugged but had the balls to at least look a bit remorseful. "Look, for what it's worth, I really liked you, Evie."

"I really liked you too, Jimmy. I considered you my younger brother. So please untie me and let me the fuck out of here," I pleaded. "If not me, then Lucy. She's truly innocent."

Jimmy snorted. "Really? Is that what you think?"

My eyebrows arched. "All of these women are innocent. Seriously? What kind of sick fuck takes women, minors, and babies against their will? I gotta tell you, Jimmy. I thought you were doing this shit because you had to. But it seems to me this is what you're into. You're just as bad as Sebastian."

"Oh sweetheart, you haven't seen anything yet." Jimmy moved quickly into my personal space and pressed his face close to mine. "Your nightmares can't compare to what I enjoy." He pulled back and brought a knife from his back pocket, then reached over and slit the knot from the ropes on my wrist. Then he bent down and did the same to my ankles. "But lucky for you, you're not the one I'm here for." He stepped back and walked over to the steel table. He crossed his arms and looked at me expectantly.

I pulled back, confused but quickly shook that off. I moved my shoulders around to get the feeling back into them. "I can go?" I shook my ankles and gauged the distance from the cot to the door.

Jimmy sighed and pinched the bridge of his nose. "Seriously. You're smarter than this. Why the fuck would I let you go now? You're leverage." He pointed to the shower. "Now wash up."

"I'm not getting in there and I'm not getting naked in front of you." Jimmy stalked over to me and moved to grab my shoulders, but I was too quick for him. Because I was sitting down, and he was standing, I had a great advantage. I quickly pulled back my fist and punched him in his nuts, with all my weight. He let an agonized wail and his hands dropped to his crotch. I quickly moved away from his reach and raced to the door, but I wasn't fast enough. He grabbed my ankle, and I fell to the ground, my head hitting the floor. As black dots danced in my vision, I started kicking him hard with my other leg. I felt, then heard, the crunch of bone. I must have broken his nose.

"Argh!" It was a garbled sound. I scurried to my feet and after faltering for a brief second, I flung open the door. I remembered I came from the left, so I ran right. I needed to find Lucy and get the fuck out of here. The hallway seemed endless. I tried several doors, but they were all locked. Finally a stair case going up appeared after I managed to open. Going up meant we were in the basement. Fuck. Without hesitation, I started clamoring up the stairs.

The sound of a door banging open made me pause. I glanced up to the open shaft and saw the head of purple box braids. "Lucy!" I whisper shouted.

"Evie! I'm up here. Come on!" she called. I hustled up the

three flights of stairs and vowed to work more on my cardio by the time I met up with her.

She handed me a rifle and with a knowing eye, said, "You know to work these, right?"

My eyes widened as I took a good look at her. "Who are you, Lucy Jamison?" She gave a short laugh and gave me a wink.

"Your best friend. Guardian angel. Whoever you want me to be. Now let's get the fuck out of here."

She showed me how to disengage the safety of the rifle, then did the same to her own. She crept silently back up the stairs with me at the ready behind her. She flung open the door on the fourth floor and we moved silently down the hall. It looked exactly like the hallway I was in previously.

"Do you know where we're going?" I asked, my voice low.

I saw her shoulders raise. "Meh. More or less."

"That doesn't bring me confidence, Lucy!"

Sounds of gunfire above us had us freezing in our spots.

"Shit. Looks like the crew is all here. We need to get the fuck out of here," Lucy yelled. Suddenly, the power shut off. "Fuck! Let's go!" We started to run, using the faint red emergency light as our beacon. It was an emergency exit, marked with an alarm warning. I could barely see her light brown skin and green eyes, but I looked at Lucy and nodded. Together, we pushed open the door. A shrill alarm rang out as we moved through. But what we thought was a door to the outside wasn't. It opened to an opened-air courtyard of sorts surrounded on all sides by brick and mortar.

My eyes went to Lucy's in fear. "Are you fucking kidding me right now?" I shouted.

"Look for an exit. A gate, vent, door. Anything!"

My gaze ran over the walls, finally landing on a door that practically blended in with the brick. We ran over and pulled on the lever. Nothing. It wouldn't give. More gunshots rang out and an explosion thundered across from us. With nothing to hide behind, we ducked down, my body covering hers. Small rocks and debris pelted us from above. More shouts and gunfire were heard but sounded further away.

I moved off Lucy, and she looked at me with fear in her eyes. "You're bleeding," she whispered and pointed to my head. I brushed my brow and saw blood on my hand. "I'm fine," I muttered. I looked around. What was a wall was no more, so I pulled Lucy to her feet and hauled her over to the blown-up area.

We climbed through the wreckage. Bodies littered the ground. Dead women in various states of undress. Men of varying ages and ethnicities. "This was the auction room," I muttered to Lucy. My eyes widened in knowing. "Shit. What did you see when you pulled out of the first room? Were there kids here?"

Lucy shook her head in thought. "I don't think so, but I would be truly surprised if there weren't. I know they were part of the last transport."

My head reared back in shock. "How do you know about the transport list? What's going on?"

Lucy sighed and picked up her rifle. "I've been working this case with the FBI for the last three years. We've been hunting the Cruz Cartel and the Syndicate with your friend Zeke." She checked her gun for damage. "Me and Roger both. Thanks for watering down Eugune's whiskey by the way; he was becoming a pain in the ass to deal with."

Completely flabbergasted, I shook my head. "Nope. I'm not going to break this down. I'm going to put this in a box and come back to this later." I picked up my rifle. "So let's go look for these kids, FBI lady."

We quickly checked the women for any sort of pulse, with no living people found.

"If this is the auction area, the kids shouldn't be too far away." We hurried into the hallway and started checking each room.

"The rooms seem like they're soundproof," Lucy mumbled.

"It's bad for business if a baby is crying while you're trying to rape women," I replied in disgust.

"Fucking bastards," she spat out. We went into the final room of the hall and tried the knob. Locked.

"Back up. Let me see if I can get this opened." She stood back and fired at the door knob. Another explosion sent shock waves through the building. "That wasn't from me!" She shouted. I went over to the door and kicked the door. After a couple tries with both mine and Lucy's leg power, we managed to get it open.

To the sounds of screams and cries. My heart melted with relief at the sight of three teenagers holding babies, with about five younger kids huddled next to them. One of the teens, a boy about the age of twelve, stood up and gave the baby to the sole teenage girl.

"You come any closer and I'll kill you!" he shouted. He raised his fists, his shaggy black hair in his eyes.

"Hey, bud. We're the good guys, I promise." I raised my hands up in surrender. He glared at me then looked at Lucy. After she nodded, he visibly relaxed.

"You guys okay? How long have you been here?" I asked over the din of the babies crying. There were three in total, at various infant stages.

The teen boy shrugged. "I don't know. We've been here for at least a day, but we were at another spot for a few days before this one." He motioned to the box across the room. "That's all our supplies. We don't have much left."

"We got you, bud. Thank you so much for taking care of them. We're going to get you out of here. Do you remember how you got in here?"

"Probably."

"Okay great. Do you think you can lead us out?"

"Yeah."

"Good. You two," I pointed to the two other teenagers, "we are going to need you guys to try and quiet the little ones, but we're walking out of here."

Lucy glanced out the door looking up and down the hall. "So far we're clear. Kid, which way?"

"My name is Jack. We came in from the right." He pointed. He picked up the oldest baby and bounced him on his hip.

"Good, that means we're not going through the auction room," I muttered. The last thing I needed to do was traumatize these kids even more. We filed out in a line, with Lucy leading the way and I bringing up the end. I was surprised we didn't see anyone lingering. It was as if they forgot about everyone they had captured, but with the sounds of chaos I could hear in the distance, that was probably a good thing.

We made it down the hall and turned a corner, then immediately stopped. One of the walls must have caved in during an explosion, and we were blocked.

"Shit. Let's turn back," Lucy swore.

A commotion behind us had us frozen in our tracks. I pushed the kids behind me and raised my weapon. Several large men came running in, with faces I recognized.. My heart swelled in relief. Cole.

"Oh thank fuck." He ran over to me and wrapped me in his arms. Cole's voice was hoarse and raspy, but hell if it didn't make my knees weak. I let my body fall into his and took in his warmth.

"About fucking time you got here," Lucy quipped.

"You were doing fine all on your own, Little Bird," the largest man replied. His bald head was covered in ink and he was dressed like the others, in black tactical gear and held a large rifle. Lucy looked at him, then looked away quickly. The man looked like he wanted to say more, but he didn't. I wanted to pull her aside, to see what was going on, but I knew this wasn't the time or the place. He lifted his chin at me in greeting. "Name is Toren. Glad to finally meet you." I nodded back, too surprised to do anything more.

"Noah and the Bravo team are taking the lead. Let's grab the kids and get the fuck out of here." Zeke replied, coming into the room. "We have incoming and feds are on their way. We need to get to the rendezvous point." He nodded to me. "Good to see you again, Evie."

I gave him a tense smile and pulled away from Cole. With the kids grouped in the middle, we surrounded the kids and moved out back into the hallway, going back the way we came. After several tense filled minutes, we finally found the exit.

They opened the door and looked outside with their weapons at the ready.

"I've been radioing ahead for transport, but they're not responding. If we take you outside right now, it's going to be open season. I'm going to run and grab the SUV I see ahead. I will be back in two minutes. Tops," Zeke said quickly to the kids. Toren and Cole took up protective positioning while Zeke ran outside. It took a bit longer than two minutes, but Toren gave the signal that he made it to safety. Soon, the large black SUV made a squealing stop in front of the door. Zeke remained in the driver's seat, while Cole maintained his position.

"Okay guys. One at a time." Toren helped one of the teens

into the car and handed her a baby. a couple of the younger kids into the vehicle. He reached out for the next kid, a young girl about the age of seven, but suddenly the brick above our head splintered from a bullet. The kids ducked behind me and Lucy, shrieking in terror.

"I really didn't want to have to damage the goods, but I guess we could always get more." Sebastian's slimy voice came from behind the horde of vile, disgusting men.

I lifted my chin and raised my weapon and trained it straight to his face. "I'm surprised you weren't among the bodies of dead men with their dicks half blown off." I gave him a scathing glare. "Pity."

Sebastian chuckled darkly. "I have to give it to you, Evie. I'm impressed. You may have had me fooled for a while. I mean, hell. You were dipping in both pools. You not only found your fortune as the Broker delivering babies and women to the Syndicate, but you also got to be the Good Samaritan and 'help' them out. Please. Tell me how it feels to be such a fucking hypocrite?"

"I was only doing what I had to do to survive. I didn't want any of this!" I roared. My voice shook.

"You didn't? While you were pretending to be compassionate and caring, you were selling human beings. I own my darkness. But what about you? What about what you gained from all of this?" Sebastian continued, taking a step toward me.

I took a step back and muttered to Lucy, "Get them the fuck out of here." She started slowly moving the kids outside.

"How the hell did you find out?" I snapped. I needed his attention to be solely on me.

"How did I find out that you were a double agent? Simple. Your husband told me." I wanted to bust that smug grin off his face.

"Thank god he's dead, or I'd kill him myself," I shot back. I always knew Maks was only interested in himself and what benefited him. It didn't necessarily shock me that he ratted me out, although I wasn't sure how he knew.

"Did you know he's alive? I didn't. Well. Until recently. But a well-placed source in the FBI alluded to the fact a Russian had been very helpful, so I had to do a bit of digging. Apparently when I asked my dear brother to take care of a problem for me, he didn't kill him like I asked. He merely staged his death. Convincingly, I must say." The group of men behind him swiftly turned around as they took fire from the incoming team, and his attention was diverted. He whirled away from me and started shooting.

Without wasting a second, I grabbed the hand of the older kid and ran out the door and into the light of day. Another shot rang out, and pain blistered through my arm. I dropped to my knees and pushed the kid to the waiting SUV. "Go!"

"Evie!" Cole's frantic voice screamed out from a distance. The SUV with the kids took off, and for a minute, I was grateful. The kids were safe and that's all that mattered. I tried to scramble to get up, but I was kicked in the stomach. Pain radiated through my side and my stomach. I couldn't breathe. I fell onto my side and rolled over to my back.

"Don't even fucking think about leaving. You destroyed my business. You thought you could run me out of this town. But I am the fucking leader of the Syndicate. I am the fucking king of the Cruz Cartel. We will be stronger than ever after this mess. The people and leverage I have over them far exceeds anything you could comprehend. You will never get away from me. And if I have to bring you to the depths of hell I am in, I will do so gladly," Sebastian seethed, ignoring the gun fire and fighting around us. He stepped through the door with his Glock pointed directly at me.

The gun fired and I closed my eyes, waiting for the pain.

But the sound of a fist fight had me open them. Cole had thrown himself on top of Sebastian, tackling him to the ground. I watched as they struggled for his weapon. I grappled for the weapon that I had dropped when it was kicked away from my grasp. I looked up and saw Jimmy standing over me with a smirk.

"Nah, Ma. Sorry. But it's my turn." He raised his own rifle, and I flinched. Waiting for him to make do on his promise and kill me.

Thwack thwack. The bullets I thought were for me, were in Sebastian's head. Cole drew back in surprise, his upper body covered in his blood.

"Cole!" I screamed. I struggled but managed to get into a sitting position. He crawled over to me and frantically checked my body for injuries. "I'm okay. My arm is on fire, and my ribs are broken, but I'm okay. Are you?"

Cole nodded, numb. His eyes started to glass over. "Cole? Cole!" I screamed. I looked over at Jimmy, as Cole slumped to the ground. "Jimmy, please! Please help me!"

Jimmy's lips thinned. "I saved your ass because you were good to me. But here's where it ends. We're on opposite teams now." He nodded to me. "Good luck. I can't promise this is the last time you see me. But I hope it is." He walked back into the fire fight without looking back.

I maneuvered Cole onto his back and looked everywhere. Above his ribs, disguised by his black T-shirt, was gunshot wound.

"Cole, No! Please wake up! Someone help us!" I screamed. The sounds of tires screeching to a stop and boots pounding the pavement came quickly. I quickly covered him with my own body.

"Evie, we got him. The medic is standing by," Zeke soothed. He bent down to pick me up, while two other men started working on Cole. My tears came quickly, and he helped me into the SUV, then loaded him into the back. I watched as two grown men helped work on their teammate in the cramped space.

I twisted in my seat to watch them, never once taking my eyes off my husband. "We're headed to the nearest trauma unit. We got the IV started, and his vitals are stable for right now. But Toren, get us there as fast as you fucking can." The blond guy with the low man bun said. He looked up at me and his green eyes twinkled. "I'm Benji. Their medic, and really, the best-looking guy on the team. But I'm sure you already knew that. Don't worry, Cole will be his normal pain-in-the ass self soon enough. He's going to milk it for all it's worth. Just warning you."

I gave him a numb but faint smile. I didn't pay attention to what he was saying. I wanted him to fix my husband. It felt like both hours and minutes, but we finally made it to the hospital. A gurney was waiting for us when we opened the doors. Benji rattled off Cole's vitals and rushed with the gurney into surgery.

Zeke helped me into a wheelchair and brought me back into the room. After two hours of being poked and prodded, Zeke filled me in.

"Toren and Lucy got the kids to the fed's rendezvous point. They're currently at a separate facility being checked out," Zeke explained. I flinched as the nurse stitched up my arm. Thankfully, I wasn't completely hit with the bullet, but it was a graze.

"What about their parents? Where did the kids come from?"

"The teenagers and older kids, they were either runaways or abducted from foster families. The babies," Zeke's face grew grim. "We believe the babies were from the Syndicate incubator farm out in Texas. The feds are going in right now and taking them down."

"What's going to happen to them?" I wondered, trying to take a breath. The x-ray told us that the ribs were fractured, and we were just waiting for them to be taped.

Zeke shrugged in defeat. "I have no clue. It's out of my jurisdiction. But the feds will make sure they're taken care of."

I sighed. There wasn't much more I could do. "When do I get to see him?"

The nurse, a woman my age with silver hair that had the nametag of Jen, looked at Zeke, then looked at me. "I know you brought him in, but I really can't release any information to someone other than family."

I smiled. "It's fine. I'm his wife. Please, what's the latest?"

Jen looked at me skeptically, then shrugged. "Fuck it, I don't get paid enough to care." She went over to the computer and within a few keystrokes, had what we needed. "According to his chart, he went in for surgery about an hour ago. Seems like it went well with a few minor complications. His left lung collapsed, so they fixed that. They removed the bullet. It looks like he's almost done and about to go into recovery."

"Can I see him?" The need to be with him was consuming my thoughts. I needed to see for myself he was good, he was safe.

Jen read a few notes, then nodded. "As soon as we get you cleaned up, wrapped up, and discharged, then yes, you can go see your husband," she said with a small grin.

Four hours later, I was sitting in Cole's recovery room. He woke briefly but had slept most of the time. My chair sat next to his bed, and my hand never left his. Exhaustion was creeping over me, so I laid my head down next to his fingers on his bed.

"Kitten." His whisper came. "I need you next to me." I

glanced up and caught his gaze. My eyes welled up with tears. I wiped the few that ran down my cheeks as I smiled at him.

"I can't, mi marido. There are too many wires. I don't want to pull anything out of you." The first time I called him my husband out loud to him. I realized I didn't have to translate when his eyes lit up and his smile grew.

"Wife. Get your fine ass up on this bed now before I put you over my knee." The low growl that came from his lips made me giggle. While it may have been the drugs, this was pure Cole coming through.

"Okay bossy, you just got out of surgery. I hardly think you can really put me over your knee." He snorted but kept quiet. "And you can barely fit on the bed, let alone add me to it."

"Wife!" He smacked the bed. "Get your ass up here now," he demanded through his clenched jaw.

I sighed. "Please give me one minute. I almost lost you. I'm not trying to kill you by disconnecting something important." I left the room to search for a nurse to assist me. A few minutes later, my favorite nurse, Jen, helped me move his wires.

"If they ask if I helped you, the answer is no." She helped him shift his body over to the right. "Don't touch any of this," she said, waving her hand over him. "He doesn't need his heart racing or blood pressure going up. So, no fooling around."

Cole smirked, his eyes growing tired. "Well, that sounds like a challenge to me."

I rolled my eyes. "There's no need to worry. It's not going to be happening."

Cole's smile grew. "We'll see."

I thanked Nurse Jen and carefully climbed into his bed. Even with him moving over, it was an awkward fit. But the need to feel him alive and next to me outweighed any discomfort. My head laid on his good shoulder and I sighed, my soul feeling at peace.

"How are you feeling?" he asked, his lips pressed against my head.

"Sore, but alive. Better now that you're awake," I murmured.

"Good. Because we have a lot to do when I get out of here," he muttered. He linked our fingers together.

My brow furrowed. "What do you mean?"

"We need to move you to Maryland. I don't know how we're going to explain Mario to Jax, but my buddy gets along with everyone so as long as Mario is not a total asshole, we should be good. And then, we need to get your marriage annulled."

"Wait. Hold up. What?"

"We have a great house, but if you want to move, we can do that too. I want a dirt bike, so we can get a piece of land and make a dirt bike track." Cole rambled on as if I didn't say a word.

"Wait. Cole. I need to tell you something." I stopped him before he went on a tangent. His grip tightened on my hand, and I squeezed him back.

"I was the Broker." The weighted confession still felt heavy on my chest.

"I know," he replied simply.

"You know?" The lump in my throat swelled and more than ever, I didn't want to see or hear his disgust.

"Yeah. Zeke confirmed it when he went through all the files you sent over," Cole said quietly. I gazed into his whiskey eyes, searching for signs of disgust or anger. But all I saw was sorrow and pain.

"I didn't want to be. I had to do it. It was the only way I could survive. God, making those calls. It fucking broke me. It killed my soul to do that. I was trying to so hard to save those..." My words came out in a rush, as tears rushed down my face.

"Hey, look at me." He raised my chin up to meet his eyes. "When I first got there, I was prepared to take the Broker. Whoever the fuck was involved with the Syndicate was going to die. Pure and simple. But honestly? I'm glad you were the broker. If you weren't, you wouldn't have been able to funnel the information to us. We wouldn't have been able to take down the transports or even had known who was involved."

"But those we didn't save..."

"We have the information on who purchased them. And we'll get them back. We can't save everyone, kitten. But I promise you, we'll try." He gently pressed his lips to mine. I heaved a heavy sigh as a tear ran down my cheek.

"Hey, look at me," Cole murmured. He lift my chin with his finger.

"It doesn't make me love you any less," he said softly. "In fact, it makes me love you even more. Do you know what I thought the first time I met you?"

"I looked amazing in my bikini?" I teased softly.

Cole smirked. "That's obvious." He pecked my lips again. "No. Your heart. You were so passionate about educating everyone about turtles, about Sayulita. The way you cared for me during the storm, and the people we helped. Your heart, your entire soul, is what convinced me to say those vows in the church."

He brushed away the tears. "Being the Broker may have damaged your soul. But it didn't break it. It didn't break who you were. You saved those kids. You almost died for those kids. Your soul isn't broken, Evie. It just needs some love. My love. And I promise that every single day for the rest of my life, I'll make sure you remember it."

Tears filled my eyes again. "Every day?" I sniffled.

"Every day."

EPILOGUE

One year later

Sunsets were always my favorite time. No matter where I was, I would make sure to take at least a minute to go outside. I needed to feel the sun on my face in order to be centered and grounded. Cole and I have taken to spending as many sunsets as possible, sitting on the porch, with me in his lap. We sometimes reflect on our day, but most of the time, we spend it in comfortable silence.

A lot has happened this year, and I'm proud of the part I played. My father was charged and indicted on numerous federal financial charges, among those being RICO, money laundering, bank fraud, and conspiracy. I was most surprised to find my father was also charged with providing support to terrorist organizations. And with my father being charged, the house of cards collapsed. Politicians and corporate executives distanced themselves from all the crimes or made their own deals. The political fallout has only started and I would bet it would continue for years to come.

Maks's death became official when his body washed up on the coast of Alabama. It was legit. His throat had been slashed, but the feds weren't looking too hard for his killers. They believed, like the rest of us, his history of double and triple crossing the Cruz Cartel and Syndicate finally caught up with him. I didn't feel any remorse or guilt. The man lost at the game of fuck around and find out.

I passed along all the information I had collected on the Syndicate's trafficking ring. Once we returned from Louisiana, I provided all the names, addresses, and photos, to the federal government. They, in turn, reached out to Tactical Redemption for their support and assistance. Cole and his team, along with the feds, have made great strides in locating the victims.

I've been providing support as much as possible, both to him and to the team. I've spent a great deal of time in therapy, trying to heal myself. I got a volunteer position at the Baltimore aquarium and have been using my business classes and bar experience to help Sketch and Cole with the admin work at Tactical Redemption. It wasn't exactly what I had anticipated doing with my life, but it's better than what I was doing previously. I get to be part of the mission and give back. I feel like I found my place in the world.

Cole's wild and crazy family had embraced me fully, to include his friends. I was able to spend a month with my Abuelita. Even Mario has adjusted to having a dog brother. Cole and I are on same page on pretty much everything. With the exception of one minor issue. He wanted another dog. I wanted another cat. We compromised and adopted a sea turtle in Sayulita.

We came to Sayulita and enjoyed spending time with my Abuelita and family. Cole's family and group of friends, which now included Lucy and Macie, arrived yesterday. Our plans were nothing but relaxing in the sun and spending time together. And of course, getting married.

The chapel where we originally said our vows was damaged in a subsequent storm, so we said our vows at sunset on the beach, surrounded by our family and friends. My dress was a simple white strapless maxi dress. Macie stood as my maid of honor, wearing a beautiful pale-yellow sundress, while Cole and his best friend, Sketch, wore white short sleeved buttons down with rolled-up khakis. My abuelita walked me down the beach and gave me away.

We repeated the vows we said eleven years before, only this time, it was official. I had a diamond on my hand and a marriage license to prove it. We danced the night away in the town square, with the town joining in our joy. Watching our families come together, after everything that happened, brought a whole new meaning to living.

I've learned what happiness and love felt like and I was so glad I found it.

I sighed as I leaned against the balcony rail, closing my eyes as the sunlight kissed my face. Our hotel room overlooked the Pacific and the breeze going through my wavy hair felt amazing.

"Dios, te ves jodidamente delicioso." I shivered, as Cole's lips caressed my ear, and started nibbling down my neck. I giggled and turned in his arms.

"You look delicious as well." I wrapped my arms around his neck and pressed my nose into his throat. I let out a moan. "Fuck, you smell delicious too."

"I know we had plans to go out to dinner tonight, but mi reina, I'd rather feast on you." His brown eyes danced as his arms loosened around my waist. I sighed and tilted my head to the side, giving my king the access he seeked. He kissed up my neck, sipping and sucking a path to my lips. He crashed his lips to mine. I gasped at the intensity and let his tongue sweep against mine. The kiss was soul encompassing and only lit my flame higher. His arms dropped from my waist, and reached under my bottom, picking me up as if I was lighter than air. He held me against him, as he turned to walk back into our room. Our kiss continued as he laid me on the bed.

"Fuck, you're a damn vision." Cole knelt at the foot of the bed. He lifted my dress and pressed his face against my bare core. "Soy un hombre hambriento, pero quiero tomarme mi tiempo para saborearte."

Cole speaking Spanish always made me hot, but when he told me that he was a starving man but wanted to take his time to savor me, arousal pooled in my center. I slowly spread my legs and traced my pussy with my finger. Cole's hungry eyes followed my finger, biting his lip when I slid inside of myself. My back arched, but I wanted more. I needed more. My finger was never enough.

But before I could slide it back, Cole grabbed my hand and slowly sucked my arousal off my finger. My breath hitched as his eyes darkened. I sat up quickly as he backed up a step. I grabbed him by his dress pants and yanked him to me. I unhooked his belt and pulled them down. As usual, he wasn't wearing boxers so I didn't have to fight with anything to get to his thick cock.

I languidly licked his length from underneath, paying special attention to each of the barbells. I teased him, sucking lightly at his bulbous head.

"Oh fuck, Evie." He groaned when I finally took him into my mouth. He reached under my hair and grasped my neck. I could only get so much in before I gagged, but I hallowed out my cheeks and took as much as I could.

"God damn you feel so damn good."

My hand reached up and gently tugged on his balls as his hips started thrusting, while my other hands slid to my pussy. My finger thrusting inside me as I bobbed on his cock, sucking as hard as I could. My core tensed and I was so close. Seeing him this undone had me at the brink.

Suddenly, he pulled out of my mouth with a pop. "I love your mouth, but damn, kitten. I need your pussy more." He stood me up and lifted my dress over my head. Then he picked me up and tossed me backward. I bounced on the bed with a yelp.

He shucked off the rest of his clothes and moved to the end of the bed. "I fucking love the way you look in my bed," He growled. He sat back on his knees and put his hands under my butt cheeks and lifted my lower half. "I said that I was starving. So, it's time for me to eat."

He pressed his face to my core and devoured me, just like he promised. His tongue danced on my clit, suckling and nibbling, before he moved to my center, where he fucked me with his tongue. I grinded pussy on his face.

"I'm so close," I whined. I could feel him smile against my skin. He reached up and started rubbing my clit, which set me off. My thighs squeezed Cole's head, as his tongue was gloriously punishing my pussy. I screamed his name as I came, harder than I did before. He didn't let anything go to waste, and when he came up for air, his face and beard were soaked.

He grabbed his thick cock and pulled in long, hard strokes. "Fuck kitten, I need you." He crawled up my body, settling in between my legs. Using one arm, Cole lifted my lower half up to him. He notched his cock at my entrance and slid in slowly.

"Fuck," he groaned. "Every time, kitten. Every single time it's pedacito de cielo. A piece of heaven. You're my everything." His thrusts were slow, at first, dragging his piercings against my G-spot. I wrapped my legs around his torso, clinging to him as he increased his rhythm. His hand snaked up and caressed my breasts before he reached up to my neck. Giving me the pressure that I craved. My core tightened. My moans became louder before I started chanting his name.

"Cole!" I keened, falling off the cliff. Cole's pace faltered, then like a man possessed, he rutted into me. My orgasm led into another as he stiffened and came with a loud roar of my name. He collapsed on top of me, our bodies a mix of cum and sweat.

"God, I fucking love you." I giggled as he gave me a bunch of messy kisses all over my face.

"I love you too," I sighed, and wiped my brow. Our breaths mingled as we laid there panting. He laid another languid kiss on my lips, nibbling my bottom lip. He rolled off me and onto his back, pulling me into him.

I sighed happily.

"What are you thinking about?" he asked softly.

"How far we've come." I snuggled into his arm, where we stayed for a good while, until our stomachs reminded us that we missed dinner.

Our relationship had been a damn lesson in heartbreak and lies. Everything we went through, everything we did, had led us to this point. Broken truths had spun webs of fear and resentment. They took away countless opportunities we could have had, wasted so many years. But we had to face the broken truths of our past before our future could be what it is.

And our future looked so amazing.

ABOUT THE AUTHOR
MELISSA HUIE

Creating Sexy Twists at Every Turn

Melissa was born and raised in Maryland, where her favorite memories took place by the Chesapeake Bay. Now she raises her family in Virginia, and loves bringing her hometown favorites into her sexy, suspenseful stories. When she's not reading or trying to corral her zoo of teenagers and animals, she can be found at the local coffee shops or breweries with her favorite people.

Melissa loves to hear from readers! She can be contacted by:

Email – authormelissahuie@gmail.com
    Website – www.authormelissahuie.com
    Facebook – www.facebook.com/authormelissahuie
    Instagram - @Author_Melissa_Huie
    Tiktok - @AuthorMelissaHuie
    BlueSky - @AuthorMelisssaHuie
    Threads - @Author_Melissa_Huie
    Goodreads – www.goodreads.com/melissa_huie

ACKNOWLEDGMENTS

I honestly don't know where to begin. After twelve long years, the Broken Road Series has come to an end. It's truly a bittersweet moment for me. I have loved and lived these characters for such a long time, that they became a part of me. I have gone through so much during the past twelve years, but these characters were constant. I really feel like I gave them their best send off.

This book, hell – this series – wouldn't have happened without the support of all of you. I'm truly blessed.

My husband and kids– Thank you so much for the encouragement and love. For the emotional support tacos, the never-ending pile of fruit snacks, and the laughs. (And to the animals of the house for providing book material. Mario is taking his royalties in the form of treats). I love you.

My amazing editor Amy Briggs – Thank you for reminding me choose a fucking tense already (Ha!) and for just being a great sounding board. Thank you for being patient and letting me be dramatic. Love you chick.

My truly inspirational and sensational sensitivity editor, Renita Lofton McKinney with A Book A Day Author Services. I love our talks, your honesty, and true mama spirit. Thank you for helping me bring my characters to life. Love you, mama.

My book designers – Robin Harper and Marisa-Rose Black. Your magic is truly remarkable. Thank you for everything.

The phenomenal photographer, Jean Maureen Woodfin,

and models Josh Sargent and Morgan Boyd for bringing my vision to life. This was the most perfect picture and I'm so glad you're on my cover!

The Jens – Jen Scott and Jen Lum. I love you. You've been my rock, my sounding board, my smack of reality, the best brunch bitches, and truly sisters.

Natacha – My sister. I love you – thanks for lending me your ear, your apartment, your company, and your cheesecake. Can't wait to see you soon.

To all my friends, family, coworkers, randos on the street that would listen when I said I was writing a series – Thank you for listening to me ramble. And for your support, your love, and your encouragement.

AND TO MY READERS: Seriously – this book is for you. There were times I wanted to quit, when I felt like my writing sucked or it didn't matter. I was so done with it all. But whenever I saw you all at book events or online, your excitement and support just kept me going. Thank you. From my the bottom of my heart, thank you.

www.ingramcontent.com/pod-product-compliance
Lightning Source LLC
Chambersburg PA
CBHW060434180626
46817CB00007B/2813